BRING US THE OLD PEOPLE

❖ ❖ ❖

BRING US THE OLD PEOPLE

❖ A Novel by Marisa Kantor Stark ❖

COFFEE HOUSE PRESS :: MINNEAPOLIS

FEB 15 1999

Coffee House Press is supported in part by a grant provided by the Minnesota State Arts Board, through an appropriation by the Minnesota State Legislature, and in part by a grant from the National Endowment for the Arts. Significant support has also been provided by The McKnight Foundation; Lannan Foundation; Jerome Foundation; Target Stores, Dayton's, and Mervyn's by the Dayton Hudson Foundation; General Mills Foundation; St. Paul Companies; Butler Family Foundation; Honeywell Foundation; Star Tribune Foundation; James R. Thorpe Found-ation; Dain Bosworth Foundation; Pentair, Inc.; the Helen L. Kuehn Fund of The Minneapolis Foundation; the law firm of Schwegman, Lundberg, Woessner & Kluth, P.A.; and many individual donors. To you and our many readers across the country, we send our thanks for your continuing support.

Coffee House Press books are available to the trade through our primary distributor, Consortium Book Sales & Distribution, 1045 Westgate Drive, Saint Paul, MN 55114. For personal orders, catalogs, or other information, write to: Coffee House Press, 27 North Fourth Street, Suite 400, Minneapolis, MN 55401.

LIBRARY OF CONGRESS CIP INFORMATION
Kantor Stark, Marisa, 1973 –
    Bring us the old people : a novel / by Marisa Kantor Stark. —1st ED.
        p.   cm.
    ISBN 1-56689-074-8 (ALK. PAPER)
    I. Title.
    PS3561.A517B75   1998
    813' .54—dc21   98-21110
                                                        CIP

10   9   8   7   6   5   4   3   2   1
first edition / first printing

for Tobe

AUTHOR ACKNOWLEDGMENTS

I want to thank the people who gave me help, encouragement, and support throughout: my mentor, Russell Banks; my agent Diana Finch of the Ellen Levine Agency; and my publisher Allan Kornblum, together with all the wonderful staff at Coffee House Press.

Also, I want to thank my parents and family and, especially, Adam, for always believing in me and this book.

1

I have to be careful what I'm saying. They're watching me now, they think I'm going to try something. All afternoon I see Karyn following me, looking around corners to make sure what I am doing. I'm in the library reading a magazine and she comes in, pretends to straighten the books. Later I'm walking down the hall, I see her disappear into a room with a tray. I tell her —Stop following me like this, and she says —Nobody's following you, Maime, I'm just doing my job, but she can't tell me. I know what's going on, I'm not stupid.

Tonight after dinner they wanted I should watch the news. Every night at six o'clock they turn on the news in the dayroom and bring the people there. Most nights I watch but not tonight, tonight my mind is with other things. I'm come to sit here in my chair outside the dayroom. Well, I think it's making them nervous I won't watch, the dayroom has all glass walls and I can see every few minutes one of the nurses looks through to me. I don't care, let them look. This is my chair, I can sit here if I want to. I have till six-thirty when it's time for bed.

I like this chair because I can watch the fish. I know these fish very well, the yellow one with the funny nose, the spotted gray one with his mouth like an O, those little clear ones what swim in a group together. There used to be also an orange with black and white stripes but he's not there now no more. One day he was in his place, he liked to hide under the shelf of the rock, and the next day I'm coming he's gone. I asked at the desk —What happened to the orange fish? and they said —It died, Maime, we flushed it down the toilet. Just like that he was gone. That's not, I think, a very nice way to die. They was talking to get another but they never did.

The fish tank is peaceful the way it sits here humming with little bubbles going in white columns to the top. The water is warm. I know because one time nobody was watching I stuck my finger in the tank and the gray fish kissed the tip with his lips so it tickled and I pulled away. Soft, warm water heated from the bottom by a blue-green light.

Where I live in the west wing everything is blue. Blue carpet, blue walls. In other places there's other colors, the east wing is yellow, the dayroom and the dining room and the library are a very bright white. This way makes it easier, you always know where you are. I see blue, I know I'm coming to my room.

At six-thirty when they come for me I'll take my bag with my things and go to my room. It has my name on the door in a little card what slides into a brass frame. They have it that way so the card can come out, they can change it if they have to if someone else takes the room. That's what the nurse told me when I asked her. Because sometimes people have to change their room or a room comes empty and a new person moves in.

I'll get ready for bed, take off my things, wash my face with the yellow soap they give me what smells like a medicine. I have a bathroom connected to my room where I wash and such. It has a bar along the wall for holding on and the toilet has a plastic seat, very tall, so I don't have to bend much to sit down on it. To me I like better just a plain toilet, I don't have no trouble sitting down, and I don't need no bars. But some people need it.

When I'm ready the nurse will bring me my pills and a glass of warm milk. I like that, the milk, it feels comfortable going down.

Then it's time to turn out the light.

2

This morning my nephew Milton was supposed to come see me. I knew he was coming, he called yesterday to tell me, but I forgot until when Karyn brought me my breakfast. She said —Don't dilly-dally this morning, Maime, you're gonna have a visitor, and I remembered it was him. My heart was like a flower shutting in. Because I don't want to see him. Anybody else I would be glad to have a visitor, I like to talk to people, but not him. I have my reasons, you will see.

It was Milton what brought me to this place. He was a very big doctor, an eye doctor, now he's retired. He lives in a big house with a swimming pool and he has seven children, all of them doctors. Well, maybe not all of them, I think one or two of them is married, one's in London, and the youngest one, Vicki, is still living in the house. That I remember from when I was living there.

He says this is a nice place. It is kosher, there are people. —It's good for you not to be alone, he all the time tells me.

MARISA KANTOR STARK

And it's close to where he is living, less than an hour he drives here to see me. One time, a few times in the week, he'll come.

—How's the Tanta today?

—I'm doing all right.

—Thought I'd come by, take you for a drive. It's a great day.

—I don't know. It looks to me a little bit cold.

—Nah, it's not cold. Look, all I have on is a T-shirt.

—But there's a wind. I see the tree blowing.

—Oh, come on, there's hardly a breeze even. Let's go, I'll sign you out.

—I don't know it's such a good idea. At least let me get a sweater.

—You don't need a sweater, Tanta. I'm telling you, it's almost seventy-five out there. We'll roll down the windows, get some air.

—Milton, I want a sweater. I won't go out without I have a sweater.

—Okay, fine. Why don't you wait here then, I'll get it for you. In your closet?

—No, I can get it.

—All right, so you get it. I'm going to sign you out.

I am past ninety, I'm a lot on his hands now. I don't like that. He's not what he used to be, he's not the same nephew what he was. He took everything from me and put me here.

3

I was born in Poland 1901 or 1902 in a little village. I was the youngest of three children. I lived through the Second World War.

The rest of my family what was still in Poland and also my husband's family was killed by the Hitlers. They took from us everything. The house, the store. Even the old people they took away. Bring us die alt war, zum Schiessen, they said. This is German. Bring us the old people so we can kill them.

MARISA KANTOR STARK

4

I wasn't always here. I used to have an apartment not far away in Newark with my husband. It was a very nice apartment. We had a long hall with rooms and a kitchen what was very big, two people could be cooking there. There was a walk-in closet by the kitchen with shelves where I was keeping the towels. Two sets of towels, white for milchig, blue for fleishig. And also a tiny room, not a room even, a place just for a table. It had a big window, in the morning the sun shined in very strong, and the birds would come to sit on the windowsill. It was very wide; I was leaving bread crumbs there.

I remember everything how it was. Always I was up early and I liked to sit by the table, drink a coffee, watch the birds. Once I saw they built a nest there. I heard a noise, I go to look, and there's two baby birds with their necks stretched up and their beaks open and the mother bird poking her beak down their throat. I stand for a long time watching while my coffee goes cold on the table. I never seen such little pink birds. Their beaks is the biggest part of them, and their eyes yet are still closed. But they know to make noise their mother should bring to them, they know already to survive. Every springtime after that they was there making another nest and when it comes April I start to watch for them. But I keep them for myself. I wasn't telling nobody not even my husband.

In front of that window is where I kept my African violets. I had different ones, purple, pink, white, they were very large with nice healthy leaves. There was six hanging from a rope in the ceiling, one under another with a wooden bead between to hold them, and some others on the window ledge. My favorite is the plant with curly white flowers what I have in a red clay pot shaped like a camel. The pot I got in Israel. It was a little market where they're making such things. The man said five shekels but I don't pay five. I know how to bargain with them. I say —This is just clay, I won't give you no more than three. He says three and a half. So I start to walk away and he calls after me —All right, all right, three shekels, but you're cheating me from my business. I come back, tell him to wrap it for me in tissue paper, it shouldn't break when I take it home. I know how to deal business.

Down the hall from the kitchen was the living room and two bedrooms. But we don't need two bedrooms, it's only me and my husband, and in one of those rooms we keep the television and the brown couch, a corduroy, with little holes in the cushions and white puffs of cotton coming out. It was very old, it was old when we bought it, very cheap, from a lady what her daughter was cleaning out her apartment. The cushions are low and flat. But my husband don't want to get rid of it. It was where he liked to sit, he would sit there in the evening, his feet on a stool cushion in front, while I'm doing what I'm doing, getting ready the supper. He never turned the light, the dark came down around him where he sat. He sat that way maybe an hour until his head is only a shadow against the window. Then I call to him and for a minute there's nothing. Then a sigh and the sound of his feet hitting the floor. Then the creak from the couch when he stands up.

The new velvet sofas with the plastic covers were in the living room. There was two of them, a long and a short, and an oval coffee table with a glass top to go between. I got them when we moved to the apartment. We moved from a smaller place, we needed new things to fill the rooms.

Because we made good in this country and we had things. Clothes and things for the house. It was not all at once, it was hard time and hard work, but we made it all right. We had our own place again.

5

Thirty-three months during the war I was hiding with my husband by a Polish man. We left the village in the middle of the night.

—Saul, we can't stay here anymore.

—Leibish asked again will we go with him.

—Tell him yes. There's nothing now to keep us.

It was less than a week from the first time he asked us. But things was entirely different. We didn't have no more our parents to think of.

Leibish was a very poor man living in the other village. He had a wife and five children and then one day he came back to the house they were gone. The Hitlers came to the village, taking the men away to work, and when they come to his house and saw he was not home they took out his family and shot them in a line against the house.

Leibish was returning to the village, the people told him —Don't go home. But he had to see it himself and what he

MARISA KANTOR STARK

saw was the neighbors taking the bodies in a pile in the cart and the women crying. After this he was become a different man, a dead man together with his family. His eyes turned to glass with nothing behind them and to look at him I saw back only my own face.

He didn't stay in that village, he ran away to my husband. He knew us because he used to buy from us in the store and also his wife was sometimes coming with one, two of the children. So he told my husband —The Germans are in my village, they're talking to round up the people to the shul. It's not long before they'll also be here.

He says he has to hide, he knows a place but he had no money. And we had the money but we had no place. So he was a help to us and we was a help to him but he was a bigger help because he had the place. He was a peddler, he spent the week going around to different places and he knew lots of people.

It was with a Polish man he was hiding us in the attic over the animals. There was goats and chickens, it smelled so bad you wouldn't believe. They was dirty people. Gott in himmel, I never saw such big lice. They was everyplace, crawling in our hair, our clothes. We had only the clothes we was wearing and no soap, maybe just a little bit of rainwater in the bucket for washing. Because when we left we couldn't be taking nothing. It was terribly dangerous, going without the yellow arm bands. The next day we heard they shot at the train twenty-eight people what was trying to escape without the bands. So we were lucky, us they didn't shoot.

We were there by that man for only a few weeks, then we had to move. The man was living with his mother, she was an old lady with rotten teeth. I couldn't stand to look at her, the teeth all brown and broken in her gums. Every Sunday she was going to church, not the man, he wasn't a churchgoer, but she would go and the priest maked to talk about the Jews. He told the people —You can't be hiding them, the Germans will find them and kill them and also you they will kill.

Because they would come to a house and burn the house with the Jews, with all the people there inside, even the children. They would stand by the doors with guns and let nobody to leave. I'm heard many times what it was, the screams while they move back in the rooms to escape the fire, pressing together to the wall with the flames at their feet. The soldiers with their faces turned away.

The old lady came home and she was talking this to her son we should leave. He came to us. —My mother, she's afraid. She says you should leave tonight when it's dark, nobody should see from where you're coming.

—You're throwing us out? Where should we go?

—I don't know where, this is a war. You go where you can find a place. If you're going to live, so you will live.

My husband was calling him all kinds of names. —He's a mamzer, listening to that woman. Both of them mamzerim. If we're going to live, he says. How can we live if he's throwing us out?

But to myself I was thinking we have to live. It can't be what we did is for nothing. Because I was young then and when you are young no matter what happens you want to live. There's something inside you what holds on and can't let go and you're always thinking what can I do to survive.

So I said to Leibish —Think, maybe you know another place.

—I don't know, Maime.

He talked very slow, he had a stutter, and the words came like with pain from his lips. He had a habit, with his thumbs he touched the places between his other fingers, one two three over and over, and I watched him. —Think. If there's one, there must be others. If you don't think, we'll all be killed.

He was sitting on the floor against the wall, very tall and thin, his clothes hanging on his body like on a wire hanger. His cheeks were sunk like pockets into his face, there was patches of gray on his chin. He was my husband's age but he looked to be much, much older.

—Stop with your fingers, already. It's making me crazy. Think.

—There is . . . there's one man.

—Yes?

—He's a shikkur, but who can say, maybe he'll help us. I heard him talk, he's not a bad man.

—Tonight, you go find out.

My husband shook his head. —Maime, are you crazy, we should trust our life to a shikkur? One night in the tavern and the whole world will know where we're hiding.

—You have someplace else, Saul, you're not telling us about?

We all know there's no other place. The Polish people are afraid of the Germans to be helping us. So at night Leibish goes out, and comes back. —Well? —It's all right, he said. —The man will take us.

He was a farmer, he had a cellar in the floor of the barn where he was keeping a few things, onions, potatoes, and he was hiding us there underground. We will pay.

We had nothing, just a very small room with a stove. If I moved around so I touched my husband. The walls were dirt with boxes of weeds and things he was growing piled up against them and there was ropes of onions hanging from the ceiling. When my husband stood up the top of his head brushed against them, they crinkled like paper and little flakes of dry red skin came down in our hair. The smell of onions was always in our nose, I knew it like the smell of air.

The floors also were dirt with some boards to sleep on and he brought us two candles for light. Sometimes he would bring me something what his wife was sewing I should work on it. And I do by that light a little bit of work. I was glad to do it, it filled the time. There's so much time, I wake up in the morning thinking on all the hours ahead to fill, try to fall back to sleep to make the day go shorter. Because in the day we were just sitting, and Leibish on those boards staring at the ceiling. Eleven hours until night again.

Only at night we're able to come out to walk and get a little bit of air. I would stand, breathe the air, throw back my head to look at the stars. In Poland, you know, the sky is darker from here, it's better to see the stars. Little points of light, like holes Gott poked in the sky. I can't hardly believe they was the same stars from before the war. How can it be, I ask, that the world isn't changed with the things they were doing. Or more, the things they made us to do. That a person can bring their parents and the stars will keep shining and shining.

In my room here on the ceiling somebody taped some stars. A nurse maybe, thinking it will be nice, or it can be whoever had this room before me asked for them to be put up, they should have to look at before they fall to sleep. I don't know who lived in this room. When I moved in, the drawers and the closet, everything was empty. I found only an emery board, too soft to use, in the second drawer under the lining paper.

MARISA KANTOR STARK

There are times at night I cannot sleep and I get up, sit on the chair by the window. It's not all black in the room, they leave a little white light burning near the bed, and in this half-dark I see the stars glowing on the ceiling. I sit very still and quiet and stare at them and I pretend I'm outside in a wide open field. But it's not easy because they don't look like stars really. They aren't moving at all. And I don't go out no more at night but I remember for certain the stars move. In and out like they are breathing.

6

My friend Berta was talking we should be glad to be here. We were sitting together in the dayroom, watching the wrestling on television. When first Berta showed me about wrestling I thought it was real and I don't want to watch but then she said —It's all pretend, Maime, come sit with me. Well, I can't see, if it's pretend, what's the point of watching, but she was by herself and I had not too much to do so I said all right. And I'm not sorry. It's very exciting really. So much action what goes on. You wouldn't know it's not real if she didn't tell you.

She starts to say something and I say —Shh, I want to hear what the man is saying. But then there's a commercial and she takes out her string from her pocket like she does to play with it, twisting it around her fingers. —You know, Maime, it's a good thing for these kinds of places. I mean, it's too much for the children to have me in the house. It's a lot of money to keep me, to have a nurse and such.

I'm not saying nothing. The commercial is a woman having aspirins. She swallows them down and her headache goes away just like that. She's an older woman with very white hair what looks to be blue, and a red pants suit. She smiles. I see she has perfect teeth. Then the commercial is over and it's coming back to the show. I'm watching the screen but I'm not thinking no more about wrestling, I'm thinking what Berta was saying. I tell you, she's not wrong about it. The old people have to be someplace, and this is not a bad place to be old. It's kosher, there are people. So I'm not alone. I have a room, it is clean, with a bed to sleep, a chair, a dresser with three drawers where I keep my things. There's a closet and one window with a blue striped curtain. The same kind of curtain like what's down the middle of the room. It's an ugly curtain, the stripes don't match to the kind of blue on the walls, but what can I do, I didn't choose it. Over the dresser is a little mirror. It's put for a taller person and I tell them the mirror is too high they should lower it but they don't listen, they never listen what I'm saying. If I want to see I have to stand on my toes.

On the dresser is one African violet. My nephew brought it to me and whenever he comes he asks —Tanta, did you remember to water the plant, the soil looks a little dry. Then he fills a paper cup from the sink in the bathroom and pours it into the pot. But he don't know nothing about plants, he don't know if you get water on the leaves of an African violet they can rot. He's doing it all wrong and then the plant never has no flowers. Every morning when I'm fixing myself I check maybe today there will be something, a little bud or something. I don't know even what color flowers it would be. I like white but who can say.

Also he hung some pictures, two children, a boy and a girl. I think his grandchildren.

In the mornings they come to my room with the breakfast, some oatmeal, maybe a bread. It's not too much, not even coffee they don't bring. They say coffee's no good for you but that's nothing, all my life I been drinking coffee. Most days it's Karyn what comes and she brings me my medicine. It used to be she was also helping me dress but now she isn't coming no more.

—What do you want to wear today, Maime? You always wear the same thing, how about something different?

—I don't have different. I have only this one clothes.

—Fiddles, that's not true. Look here in the closet, all these clothes. How about this brown dress? It's a real nice material.

—No, that one I don't like. It makes me look like a tent.

—How's it gonna make you look like a tent? You're so little.

—I tell you, it makes me wide like a tent. I won't wear it.

—Well, then how about this one? Skirt and top, it makes a nice outfit.

—No, it has short sleeves. I'll be cold.

—Okeydoke, you win. Wear the flowered dress again if that's what you like.

—Don't tell me what to wear. I can get dressed by myself.

It's not easy, my hands are shaking. That nurse is an anti-Semite, she don't come no more to help me. She thinks because I'm walking and talking I can do by myself and I don't need no help like the others. But to tie my shoes. You should see the time it takes me.

There's another lady in my room what she don't talk, she don't know nothing. She lies in the bed on the other side of the curtain, sometimes with her clothes on sometimes with her clothes off. She makes a noise, a moaning sound like she has a pain somewhere, and at night it disturbs me. I call the nurse they should come and pat her till she's quiet.

MARISA KANTOR STARK

In the daytime they're taking her to another room, they have a place where they put such people. Some people is saying she has a daughter but I don't see her, I don't know. I don't go to that room, even to walk past it has a bad smell like the bathroom in a train station. But I hear them talking. —Such a good daughter, she takes such good care of her mother.

—But it's all for nothing, her mother don't know nothing. If she comes if she don't come, there's no difference.

So that's how it is. I'm talking to Berta I'm thinking without it here I would be also like that woman. I would be going hungry and naked.

7

One night I was home at my apartment and I had a headache. It was after my husband died and I was alone. So I cooked myself an egg. When my husband was alive I cooked, but after it was only me I don't bother no more to make nothing fancy. I mean what will I do with it if I cook a chicken, I can't eat a whole chicken by myself. A scrambled egg is fine with a piece of bread.

After supper I was thinking I'll lie down a little bit, close my eyes, maybe it will help the headache. Then I didn't know but I fell asleep. And I was forgetting to turn the gas off by the stove.

Suddenly there was a banging on the door, somebody rattling the door knob. —Maime, are you there, let me in. What, what is it. I jump from the bed, dizzy. It was Lou, what she was living upstairs with her husband Herman, standing in the hallway in her checkered bathrobe.

—Lou, what happened, what's the matter? Are you all right?

—I smelled gas, Maime. It's coming up to my apartment through the radiator.

She pushed past me into the apartment and goes into the kitchen. —My God, Maime, look what you did. You left the gas on.

She turned it off and opened the window and pulled me back to the hall. We was standing there, her in her bathrobe and me in that old brown housecoat what I'm wearing around the apartment. It was torn at the elbow, I never let nobody see me in that housecoat, and my hair was a mess.

—I was sleeping.

—I know you were sleeping. What if I didn't find you, you could have been poisoned.

—It was nothing, a little headache. I would have waked up.

—Come upstairs with me.

—Like this? I don't go no place looking like this. You come inside, I'll fix myself a little bit. Maybe make some coffee.

—You can't go in there, Maime, you'll pass out. We'll have coffee upstairs.

—But like this . . . I don't even have my shoes.

—You don't need your shoes, slippers are fine. Come on now.

She called my nephew. I told her she don't have to but she wasn't listening.

—What's his number?

—Lou, please, I just closed my eyes a few minutes.

—I'm sorry, Maime, I have to call him. What's the number?

—It was nothing.

—Maime.

—I don't know. I have it someplace written down.

—Where does he live? I'll call information.

Milton came. He was talking to Lou so I can't hear what they're saying. I was in the same room with them but they were talking too fast and soft, I can't make the words. I said

—Milton, what you're saying, I don't understand you, and he said —I was saying I think you should come stay at my house for a while, Tanta. I don't like to leave you here alone.

I try to tell him this isn't necessary, not at all, but he won't listen to nothing. He said he was thinking for a while already I shouldn't be by myself, the neighborhood was changing and it wasn't safe no more for a woman alone. —Just for a few days, anyway, till we decide what to do, he told me.

What's to decide.

I went with him but I wasn't happy there. He has a nice place but it's not for me, it's not what I'm used to. The house is very big in a fancy neighborhood with two stone lions in front. Across the street they also have such lions, it must be there was a sale. There is a gardener what comes around and plants by the houses all the same red and white flowers with little stones. And next to the pool is a tennis court with lights on it. Debbie plays very good tennis, and all his children play. Well, I don't play. I didn't play tennis a day in my life.

I sit all day in the chair and if she's cooking something in the kitchen I go in, I'm thinking to help her. But she says —No, no, there's nothing to do. Really, I'm not doing anything. Just sit and relax. So I go back to the chair or I take a walk around and then she calls me to the table, there is the supper. Even the bed in the morning she was making for me. I had a room with a pink flowered bedspread and a bathroom what matched. It had a pink bathtub and Debbie hung there little pink and green and white towels in a gold hoop. She said they was for decoration, there was another towel to dry with. —See, Tanta, first-class accommodations. We love to have you. Every morning she put a fresh towel. This is not a life.

His daughter Vicki was all the time in and out, having her friends. To me it's nothing how she does. It's not my business, she's not my daughter. But every day I see her I tell my nephew it's time she should meet some Jewish people. She's twenty-three, twenty-four, I was already married. I know she goes away in the summer to the mountains where there aren't no Jewish people. I say to her. —Where you will get kosher food? and she don't answer me. She knows what is kosher. Because I told her —During the Second World War we were hiding thirty-three months by a Polish man and there weren't no kosher dishes.

I kept asking Milton when I'm going back to my own apartment. It was more than a week and then finally he said —All right, today I'll take you back. But when we got there, before I can get my key from my bag even, a woman I never seen before opened the door. She was a black woman like Karyn but much younger and slimmer, she looked like a girl. She was wearing jeans and a red T-shirt with a very big Mickey Mouse. She smiled at me, took my hand.

—Maime. My name's Adele. I've been watching for you.

I looked at her. —I think there's some mistake. This is my apartment here.

My nephew took my arm and led me inside. —Tanta, Adele's going to stay with you for a while. She'll help you around the house, be some company.

—Thank you very much, I don't want no company. It's nice to meet you, Adele, you can go now.

—Come on, Tanta, that's no way to behave. Here, why don't we all sit down.

The girl and him sat on the sofa. I don't sit.

—Now listen, Tanta. I worry about you all the time by yourself.

—I'm sorry you worry. Nobody told you to worry.

—I'm sure you must get lonesome sometimes.

—No. I don't.

—Well, it's not healthy to be all day in an empty house. All I ask is you give this arrangement a try. For me. Adele is a very nice young woman.

—There's no place for her to sleep. I don't have no extra beds. She can't stay here without there's a place to sleep.

—That's all taken care of. I opened the couch in the room with the television. She'll be very comfortable.

He smiled at the girl and she smiled back. —You'll see, Maime, we'll have fun, she said to me. —Do you play poker?

—No.

—I'll teach you. I brought some cards.

Poker I found is a very hard game. She likes it because she was always winning. Well, that's no surprise, she knew all the hands. She maked me a card with the different rules written on it but what kind of fun is a game you have to keep looking at a card to see what to do. So I stopped looking, I made whatever kind of hand I felt like, and then when she said —What is that, Maime, that's not a hand, I said —What makes you the boss, to me it's a hand. After two days she stopped asking will I play poker.

You wouldn't believe this woman. She was in the apartment four days and the things she was doing I could talk for weeks. She started with the soaps.

—Adele, do you know what happened to my soaps? I had extra soaps in the bathroom.

—I know, you had three extra ones on the sink. I put them in the closet.

—Why you did that?

—Well, because we don't need four bars of soap for two people. When this one's gone I'll put out another.

—I have them on the sink for a reason. That way I know when I'm running low and I need to buy more.

—Why can't you check in the closet?

—Because I'll forget to look in the closet then one day I'll run out of soap. But I don't see I have to explain this to you. This is my house, my soaps, I can put them where I want. If I want thirty soaps on the sink I will have thirty soaps and that's all.

Then I had a very nice china teapot what somebody was giving me and I noticed suddenly it disappeared. She said she threw it away, it was cracked, but twelve years I had it and it was cracked, that don't mean she can throw it away. It reminds me of a tea set I had when I was a little girl back in Poland. I make her go out to the garbage and find it. Clean it up and put it back to the cabinet where it belongs.

I also see she is cutting my violets. She calls it trimming but every time I pass by the window they're getting smaller and I know she's killing them. This I won't stand to, somebody killing my plants. I told her —My plants are like my children, you don't touch them. You understand? She said yes, yes, she understands.

But the last thing was the supper. Eggs, she was saying, is not a supper, she'll fix us something, some chicken. So she got kosher chicken like I told her and all afternoon she was cooking but then when I sit down to eat I see there is toothpicks in it. I poked it with my knife.

—What are these toothpicks in my supper?

—That's how you make it, to hold it together. It's a very fancy dish they serve at the restaurants.

She calls it a chicken kiev. Well, I don't care what name you have, I won't eat chicken with toothpicks in it. So she ate her piece and wrapped mine up in tinfoil, put it in the freezer. She said she'll eat it herself for lunch. I told my nephew —Milton, I won't have this woman in my house.

—You hardly gave her a chance, Tanta. She was doomed from the start.

What's he talking about now. I never heard that word, doomed. Why he can't use normal words.

—She isn't doomed. She's trouble. She tried to choke me putting toothpicks in my chicken. I had to eat toast for supper.

He laughed.

—What's so funny? I don't think it's funny.

—Nothing. You're right, it isn't funny. Well, maybe someone else will be better. Someone a little older.

—No. I won't have it.

—Tanta, I can't leave you by yourself. You saw what happened.

—What happened? It was nothing. For a minute so I closed my eyes. You never close your eyes? It can happen to anybody.

—Tanta . . .

—There's nothing to say more, Milton. I'm finished talking.

8

He brought me again to his house. I can't say how long I was
there. I didn't realize first what was happening, I thought it's
just another visit. But then he started bringing my clothes, he
cleaned out the apartment. A truck came to the house and I
recognize it was my furniture. The velvet sofas with the green
pillows what I maked myself and the coffee table from the living room. When company's come I was always putting out
those pillows. When he came I put them out.

So now I see he's taking it all for his house. He said it's a
shame to throw it out, it makes such nice memories. I know
all along that's how he was thinking. He was separating it out,
giving things to his children what are married. And also my
husband's suits he took. I saw him wearing a gray suit and I
remember my husband had such a suit. So I know he took it.
But I don't know what he did with my plants. His wife is not
too much with plants and I tell you he certainly don't know
nothing to take care of them. That gardener does everything.

He came to me once. —Tanta, I found a rock in your freezer.

—That's not a rock, Milton. It's a bread.

—Bread? It's very old bread.

—Yes. I put it there when we moved to the apartment.

—Thirty years ago? Why on earth are you keeping it?

Because in Poland people move to a new place so they take a piece of bread, sugar, and salt and put them all together for good luck. You have to keep it always in the house, you should have mazal there, and me and my husband did like this when we moved from the village to the town and then again when we came to this country. But my nephew is an American person. He don't understand these kind of things.

—Also I found some addresses. You want them?

—Yes, I want.

These are my good friends, my friend Raisa from Poland what she went to Israel after the war. She survived the war but she wasn't hiding like me and my husband. She was in a camp. She had a very round face with full red cheeks and she looked to be very healthy, and when the Germans was deciding who will work who will be killed, they called this cleaning the camp, she looked strong and they gave her to work. All during the war she worked in a factory in the camp. She told me how she used to trade a piece of bread for a cigarette and then that cigarette she traded to another man for two pieces of bread. That's how she lived.

She has a son Benjamin what also lived through. They weren't together, he was seven years old when the Germans took them on the train, and Raisa pushed him out from the window. She knew where that train was taking them, she said, it was her only chance. People was doing these things with the

MARISA KANTOR STARK

children, it was like the old people, they didn't have what to do with them. Sometimes there's a miracle and they survive. Gott was good to her, somebody found him and they brought him to a nun what hid him in the hospital till after the war. Raisa came back to find him after the war.

They live in Netanya, I have the address and the phone number. Her son is married, he has two grown children. Raisa was telling me every month since the war ends he is sending money to the nun in Poland. That's how it should be, Raisa has a good son. I would have done like that for the man what was hiding us, but my husband didn't want. She's terribly old now, the nun. Raisa said her son is thinking to go back to Poland and see her again before she dies.

Raisa is my dear friend. All the years we was writing letters.

Once I asked her what happened to her parents in the war. I remember them from when we were young, her mother had the same round face from Raisa and she was a cheerful woman, always laughing. When she laughed she had a dimple here on her forehead. I never know somebody has a dimple there. I used to wish I can have one.

They was killed in the camp. That's all what I know, all what Raisa was saying. They were too old to work, she said, and so they was killed. I want to ask her were you with them, did you bring them there, but I don't ask. I don't tell her, she don't tell me. Other things about the war we're talking but not about our parents.

9

When I was young if my mother should die I will want to go with her.

I come from a very religious home. My mother was a very religious woman. On Pesach we were changing all the pots and dishes it should be kosher, not touching nothing. We had a whole set of dishes special just for Pesach.

In Poland we lived in a little village, my parents, my grandfather, sister, brother, and me. There was seven, eight families in that village but we was the only Jewish people. The next village was three and a half miles walking, where we went to school, the Polish school and to cheder. That's how it was, all around villages.

My father was not a businessman. He was a scholar, he liked to sit and learn, and also he did some planting. So he built a house in the village, he thought there wasn't Jewish people there he'll make a good business. He had a plot, a block of land where he was planting different weeds, lima beans, carrots, corns, and he was thinking to sell to people. But he wasn't too much successful.

So my mother maked there a grocery. She was making good, she sold things what the people have to buy, but she sold it cheaper and they came from the village and the other villages. Without that grocery we would have nothing, we'd be like those families of poor farmers what don't have even a fur coat for the winter. My father used to joke from it, if it wasn't for my mother he'll be living in a barn. But with the money what she made he built a beautiful home. It was the biggest house in the village.

When I was born my mother was very sick. I was born at home on Yom Kippur, the holiest day in the year for the Jewish people, and my mother wouldn't send for the doctor. So I was born there in the bed and for two months after she was staying in that bed. They tied red ribbons on the posts to keep away the devil. She was terribly weak, she wasn't a big woman, very thin with small, delicate bones. My father and my sister Lia cared for her there in the house. Lia was eight years old when I was born and she worked the store for my mother.

After my mother was stronger she left me to go to America. My father was gone first to make money but he wasn't a businessman and he came back to Poland. Then my mother went and with her it was different. For more than two years she worked like a seamstress for some people. Because she knew very good to sew, always she maked all the clothes for me and my sister. Skirts, blouses, different dresses. There was one my favorite with red and green buttons down the front and pockets shaped like apples.

She left me with Lia and Lia was my mother. There was an old Gentile woman from the village what came to the house every day to help with the cleaning, maybe do a little bit of baking. She was very honest and my mother trusted her. But it was Lia what took care of me those years. She was washing me, dressing me, combing my hair. I had long red hair but it was always with knots and I cried so she left me be. So then it was always with knots.

I was three years old when my mother came home. She brought me a doll with a pink dress and umbrella and a hat with long pink ribbons. I never seen such a doll. She was standing in the doorway holding her arms out to me like this and she called me —Maimela, come to me. But I don't know her and I wouldn't go. I was only three but I remember this very clearly, how she was a stranger to me and I didn't want to go to her. She had a gold tooth in the front side of her mouth and when she smiled I saw it shining and I stayed back. I didn't recognize nobody else what had such a tooth.

I went instead to my sister and hid my face in her skirt. I was crying and she put her arms around to hold me. That's why I'm so little, you know, I'm not five feet. Because my mother left me with my sister and I did not have the milk to drink. So I didn't grow. When I'm sitting here on this chair my toes don't even touch to the floor.

When I was little my brother was terribly sick. He was at home in the bed, they couldn't move him, and he was coughing blood. I would hear him there behind the door, I wasn't allowed to go inside but my mother was passing with sheets and towels and I saw they was stained with blood. My mother was a very good doctor, and she used to take care of us when

MARISA KANTOR STARK

we was sick. She would make hot water, bring it to a boil with a little bit of milk we should drink it, but this with my brother didn't work and she went to the town for the doctor.

He came to the house, he was a very tall man and I was afraid of him. His head was almost to the ceiling and he don't look down, I can't never see his face. It was like to me he was a man without a face. I didn't understand much what was happening, only my brother was shut away and the house was quiet and my parents not paying to me no attention, always looking on top my head and talking in a fast quiet voice. If I disappeared, I thought, they wouldn't never miss me. Then I started thinking maybe I am already disappeared, that's why they don't see me, and I was walking softly through the halls in my bare woolen stockings and pretending like I'm not there. Because that will show them something if suddenly they're looking and I'm gone.

Then slowly my brother got better. The doctor said if he wasn't strong he would have died, but he was a big boy, a bit heavy even, and it was that what saved him. So always my parents worried I should be strong. —Eat, Maimela, look at you. You're so little. My mother made me little corn cakes with raisin faces I should eat.

From my mother I learned many things. I learned to sew, she would give me a little piece of cloth from what she was making, not a good piece but a scrap what was too small to use, and she threaded the needle to show me. —This stitch is like a dot and this one, this one's different, see, like an x. I sewed clothes for the dolls we made. For the woman I sewed a dress and for the man, oh, I don't know, some shirt and pants. A coat if there was enough.

The dolls were from apples. Me and my sister took them and cut with the knife a face, holes for the eyes, a nose, a small smiling mouth. Then we hanged the apples in the pantry with the jam and the pickle jars for many weeks until they got old. The pantry smelled sweet like those apples, I liked to go inside there and stand in the dark and breathe the thick smell like cider. When they got old the apples were brown and they have wrinkles like old people's faces around the eyes and mouth. Then we was taking them down and making bodies out of cloth and stuffing the bodies with rags. I made hair from white or gray yarn.

I remember one day Anyushka, she was the name of the woman what was working in the house, was going into the pantry and she saw there the apples hanging. So she was thinking they're people's heads or something else. She was a Polish woman and she was not educated, from a poor family, and she had all kinds of funny ways like that. Like when she made jam she put on top of the jar a nail to scare away the ghosts.

Well, when she saw those heads she screamed and my mother was come running. —Anyushka, what's the matter, who's hurting you? She don't say nothing but she was shaking and crying, pointing at the apples. My mother called to me —Maimela, come take down these apples, they're upsetting Anyushka. I was laughing, I thought it was very funny, but she says —Stop laughing, control yourself and behave like a mensch. But then when Anyushka turned her back away my mother also smiled and she winked at me. So like me she thought it was funny. A mother, you know, is the best kind of friend.

MARISA KANTOR STARK

She used to play games with me. We played store, I had a grocery and she was coming to buy. I would line things on the table, potatoes, soap, yarn, and I helped her to find something, like I saw her doing for her real customers. She gave me some coins to pay.

Or sometimes we played I was a grown-up guest coming to a party. I put on her clothes and her shoes, maybe also she was letting me wear her jewelry, and then I knock at the door outside. I had a little set of china with a teapot, cups, saucers, plates, all with blue and yellow flowers around the edges, and she would invite me —Come inside, we'll have a coffee. She poured it into the cups, very black coffee with a little bit of milk like we was drinking it, and on the plate she put a cookie, raisin or almond. There was only room for one cookie, it was a very little plate, so we shared it, half for me and half for her, but always she broke it so I can have the bigger piece and with the most raisins. Then we sat together at the table eating the cookie with little bites it should last longer, and talking.

Those were special times, when my brother and sister was away from the house busy with their own things, and it was just me and my mother. I remember one afternoon when she did my ears. We was home alone and she was taking the needle from the sewing and put it in the fire it should be clean. Then she put the thread in, a very thin white thread, and very fast she pushes it through my ear. I don't feel nothing because she put ice I shouldn't feel, but later at night when I'm lying in bed it hurts me and I go to her.

—Momma, when can I take the thread out?

—Not for some weeks. You have to wait until it will heal.

—Then I can have earrings?

—Yes. I will give you your first pair of earrings.

They was little gold hoops with a little chip of diamond what she was buying and saving for me. I wore them all the time even when I'm sleeping and one of the diamonds was lost. I cried when I lost it and she said —Stop, you are being foolish, there are other things worse to cry about. So now I wear only these plain gold posts what you see.

I thought it was the nicest thing in the world to be the youngest child and have parties with my mother and I worried what if some day I'm not the youngest no more, if I catch up to Lia or even become older from her. I told this to her once and she laughed at me. —You silly, you'll never be as old as me, you're always the baby. Well, I don't see how she can know for sure but she sounded like she knows and I always listened what she said so I feel better.

I don't know what happened to those little dishes from our parties. I can't remember breaking none but slowly over the years there was less and less pieces until I only had one cup and two saucers with the flowers worn away. But by that time I was not a child. I didn't care no more for those kinds of games and the cup and saucers was packed away in a box.

MARISA KANTOR STARK

10

My parents talked to me in Jewish. At school I learned to talk Polish and to the neighbors I was talking, but at home Jewish. That is my language, all my life I'm keeping the language of my parents. Only if my father was talking to my mother I shouldn't understand, then he talked something in Hebrew. I was listening to him, I'd stand outside the door where they were talking, they shouldn't notice me, and some things I pick up. That's the child I was, always wanting to know what people was saying and to understand.

❊ ❊ ❊

My father was a learned man. He was getting up early when it was still dark, maybe 4:30 in the morning, and davening all the tehillim. He maked a little candle. So sometimes I heard him get up then I get out of bed and stand by him while he davens. He gave me what prayers to say I should learn. Not at one time together but first a little bit and then a little bit. Like one day from hodu to yishtabach, from yishtabach to modim, from modim to aleinu. Then from hodu to modim, modim to aleinu. Then from hodu to aleinu. This way I learned all the prayers in the siddur by heart.

Now I'm forgetful, I need to read in the book. But it was once I knew all the siddur by heart.

My grandfather, my father's father what was living by us in the house, he was also davening all the tehillim by heart like my father. He was terribly old, not saying much and always in Jewish, but he had a very good memory. No matter what time I got up already he was awake, sitting on a bench against the wall in the kitchen like he was a part of the room. He sat there until the whole family was awake, like he was waiting to make sure were we all still there, and then he put on his coat and hat and went out. He took long walks in the village, maybe two hours, and he didn't use nothing, not a cane or nothing. He was a very strong man right until he died.

Sometimes I would sit with him and he was telling me stories about the time when he was a boy living in the village. —There was no road going between the villages, he said, —and when it snows you can be lost in the fields. Once I was lost for two days, until a stork came out from the sky and took me up in his beak and carried me home.

I ask my mother is that true what he's telling me but she just gives a little smile. —I can't say, Maimela. You never know.

I had two grandfathers what they both lived past ninety. The other one lived with my mother's sister in another village and his mind was very confused. He was waking up at twelve, davening, not knowing was it the day or was it the night. But he knew to come to the house. So sometimes he was come to

MARISA KANTOR STARK

see us, bringing me a stone what he found on the way, licking his finger and rubbing it to make it shine. He sat with my other grandfather, talking in Jewish about the pain he gets in his side.

Before I went to school my father taught me at home. He had a special chair in the corner of the big room where he would sit and learn and I sat by him so we can study together. I loved to learn with my father. He had very old books from his grandfather what he kept there on a shelf, made from a parchment with dark leather covers. The pages were yellow and crumbling at the edges and the letters were written by hand, there was a scribe what it was his job to paint each letter perfect with a brush.

I followed my father's finger moving under the letters, first to read in the Hebrew, then to translate into Jewish. His finger was thick with a square nail, his whole hand was square and strong with cracks in the skin from working the earth. Sometimes there was dirt in the cracks but never he touched the books without first he scrubbed them and when I sat by him there was the new fresh smell of soap mixed with the dusty smell from the books. When I think of my father I think always first of his hands.

My father didn't want just to read, he wanted I should think about what we was studying. —Do you think the chumash is only a storybook? he asked me. —The stories are here for a reason.

There was many stories my father read to me but it was the story of the akeida what made to me the biggest impression. I was still a little girl when he was reading it to me, maybe five years old, but I was fascinated by that story.

—Tell me, Maimela, what do you think. Why would Avraham bring his own son to be killed like that?

—I don't know. There wasn't a choice for him.

—Why no?

—Well, because Gott told him to do it. It's a test if he loves Gott.

—Is this right, do you think? Why would Gott make this test?

—He'll make it because . . . I don't know. I don't know why, I'm not Gott.

—No, you're right, we are not Gott.

—Tate, did Yitzchak know where they were going?

—The chumash doesn't tell us if he knew. But I think yes, he knew.

—So why did he go?

—I cannot explain to you why.

—Why can't you? I want to know.

He shook his head. —I just can't, Maimela. It's one of those things.

It is the first time I remember my father couldn't answer my questions.

He gave me candy when we studied together, the taste of Torah should be sweet on my lips, he said. It was a sugar candy what we make at home. Very easy to do. He took a piece of string and put it in a cup with water and some spoons of sugar. Then he leaves it on the windowsill and over the days the sugar was getting hard around the string. It makes different kinds of shapes and he would take it out from the cup and give it to me to suck on. —Look, Tate, this one is a castle with two towers. There's a princess trapped in the tower and I'm going

MARISA KANTOR STARK

to suck it away and set her free. The crystals would melt on my tongue and when they got smaller I chewed on them. —Be careful, Maimela, you don't break your teeth. My mother hated the sound from me cracking the hard candy.

Once I swallowed the piece of string by a mistake and I was thinking something is going to happen to me but my father says not to worry. He said people swallow all kinds of things, nothing comes from it.

—I probably shouldn't tell you this, Maimela, but when I was a boy I swallowed a live fish just because somebody dared me to do it.

—No, Tate, I don't believe it. A fish?

—It was a little fish. But for days I was sure I felt it flopping around in my stomach and I thought something terrible would happen to me. But you see I survived.

My mother brought home sometimes a live fish, a whitefish or a carp, and it would swim around in the bucket until she was ready to cook it, then she was cutting it open on a wooden block, her white hands in to the wrist with scales and blood. Before they died I watched how they twist around and around on the block looking for air. I thought of my father holding up such a wiggling fish.

Suddenly I saw him all in a new way. I realized there's a time he had another life, when he wasn't my father and he did things the man who is my father would never do. And I didn't like this. It was like something in my world was moved from its place. Like the day I was come home and found my mother changed around the furniture, what had been standing in the same way around the big room from as long as I remembered.

11

Later I went to school. When I was younger, before the accident, I was walking with my brother the three and a half miles. We left early in the morning, in the winter it was still very dark. The other houses were all quiet and closed up to themselves, the people inside doing what they was doing. My mother gave us hot coffee and we started with our lunch in the pail.

There was something about walking then, the cold makes things brighter and the drops of ice on my eyelashes when I blink was turned to tears. I feel the blood moving in my arms and legs and I want to run, it's hard for me to keep back my steps to match with my brother. Because he walked long slow steps and he don't talk to me much, he wasn't liking talk in the morning. But I liked to talk and then he'd turn to me. —Stop chattering, Maime, enough already. Or to tell me —Watch where you're stepping, you'll get it all over your boots.

It was only one road, a dirt road that curled around through the fields and went through the different villages. We used to

MARISA KANTOR STARK

pass the milkman going from the village where he was leaving the fresh milk at the houses and taking away the empty glass bottles. On some days his back was bothering him and then one of his sons instead was driving the wagon. He had three sons but if it was the youngest one, Yaakov, then he called to us —Jump up, I'll ride you part of the way. He was friends with my brother. I would sit between them on the wooden bench behind the horse, crowded tight against my brother, his elbow pressed in my side. I breathed in the leather smell from his coat and listened to the sound of the horses' feet on the frozen road and the rattling in the back of the wagon from the bottles. The horse's breath is coming in great white clouds. It was too cold to think. I was floating there in a kind of dream.

In the morning we was going to the Polish school, there wasn't a lot of Jewish people. Maybe three Jewish people at the whole school and all of them from a different place so we couldn't be going together. I had friends with the Gentiles, you have to be friends, but I was always feeling myself apart. We're only school friends, maybe sitting together in the yard or doing help with the schoolwork, but never more than this, never after school. I don't go to their house, they don't come to me. Because I know they're not my kind and all over the world there are anti-Semites.

But in the afternoon I went to cheder and there it was all Jewish people. We was learning boys and girls together, we sat at a long table and in the back of the room there was a fire. We learned in Jewish with a little bit of Hebrew. The boys were learning chumash with rashi, the girls only chumash.

So I am sitting and learning and the rebbe asks the boys. Then when they don't know, I know because I'm learning with my father and I say the answer. He would come over to me and hit me on the arm with his stick. But not hard, just gently like this for answering when he asked the boys. And also I wore short sleeves, only to here, and he didn't like that, he was very religious, a chassid, and he wanted they should cover the elbow. So again he was hitting me on the arm. I didn't tell it to my parents because I know they will tell me follow what the rebbe says.

Always we were going boys and girls together. We went in a group, like for Shabbos we take turns going to this one's house or that one's house, sitting around in a circle, talking and singing z'mirot. If they come to our house so my mother would bake something I should treat my friends. Then other times I stayed there in the other village by my girlfriend Raisa and later she'd walk me home. Or another one would, one of the boys. Each girl had her own special one to walk with her, maybe holding hands. Because it was good, not like there's some saying a girl shouldn't hold a boy's hand.

Shabbos in my house was the most special time. Already on Wednesday afternoon we were preparing, my mother making the challahs and I was helping her. She saved for me a little piece of the dough and I watched how she's doing then I make my own.

We waited until it was raised in bowls on the table, round hills of soft white dough like a baby's skin growing over the edge of the bowl, and then we was sticking our hands inside. It was warm and sticky, closing in around my fingers. I remember what it smelled, the sour smell from the yeast, and the flour dust on my mother's hands when she was working

MARISA KANTOR STARK

the dough. A long time she would knead it, always standing up, leaning her whole weight into the table and pushing down from her shoulders so her palms left marks in the dough. The kitchen was hot and her hair fell down from the top of her head. She had red hair like me but it was darker and sometimes there was flour also in her hair.

When it was ready we maked the dough into ropes. First my mother took a pinch and put it to the side, that was the special challah piece and we won't be using it, she burned it black in the oven. Then we did the braids. My mother had six ropes, sometimes eight, and she made such a fancy braid but I can do only a very simple one with three. I stand next to her and watch how she's doing it or sometimes I get tired and sit on the floor next to her feet. Her skirt came down almost to cover them but I see the skin is hard and peeling on her heels and dark on the bottom from walking without shoes. After it was braided we're dipping our fingers in the eggs and spreading it on the dough. Wet shiny dough, it baked into gorgeous challahs. Later at the table my father would break off the pieces and sprinkle them with salt then he was throwing them to us. With his hands, never he used a knife.

Sometimes my mother put poppy seeds in the dough or even raisins. I was picking the raisins, eating them, and she slapped my hand. —Maime, stop, there'll be nothing left for the bread. But when she wasn't looking I took another one. I love raisins. My father hated them and he poked them out from the bread with his finger. —Here, Maimela, here's another one. He put them in a line on the edge of my plate.

＊ ＊ ＊

All week we was looking forward to Shabbos and even on Sunday or Monday if my father wanted to hurry us with something he'd say —Maher Shabbat, it's almost Shabbos. When it comes Friday afternoon everything stopped. My mother was closing the grocery early and we got washed and dressed in nice clothes. When I was young I had a lot of nice clothes my mother made. Then my father and grandfather and my brother was davening Kabbalos Shabbos in the house, it was too far to walk to the shul at night. But in the morning on Saturday they walked and some weeks if it wasn't hot or too cold I was going with them with my sister or my mother. We sat there behind the curtain.

It wasn't too many women what came to the shul, mostly older women. When I was younger sometimes I went with my father. He had his place to stand and daven and all the men around davening, not together but everyone his own way like a roar of sound what has no words. When they're reading Torah so they had three four bimahs where they're reading, not like in America there's only one, and at each one people standing around, every man should have an aliya. Because this is a great honor, to be called up to the table where they are reading. I would go with my father. My head was against his stomach and I smelled his shirt and the smell from men crowded together.

But then one day my mother said —You're getting too old now, Maimela, to sit with the men, and after that I sat always behind the curtain. The curtain was a heavy gauze, we couldn't see much what was going on. There was a lot of talking. Most of the women was never gone to cheder, they don't know to daven, and they're come to the shul to see friends and to talk.

MARISA KANTOR STARK

Friday night my mother was benching leicht. She had two tall candles and I stood by her when she lit them. She would cover her head with a long white cloth what fell down to her waist and her hands over her face. Then she made the brocha —asher kidshanu b'mitzvostuv v'tzivanu l'hadlicht ner Shabbos. After this she would stand quiet with her hands over her eyes and her lips moving, slim and white like the candles.

—Momma, now what are you saying?

—Shh . . .

—Momma?

She takes down her hands. —I'm talking to Gott. This time after lighting the candles the gates of heaven are open special to the women.

—What are you talking to him about?

—That's a secret. When you're older you also will light. Then you will know.

I slipped in under the veil and she put her arm around me. In the dark I lean back into her body. I feel the warm from inside her arm on my cheek.

I had two brass candlesticks for Shabbos what my nephew gave me when I came to this country and always on Friday night I was lighting. During the week I kept them on the kitchen counter on the side of the sink by the bread box. But just the other day I realize I don't see them now no more. It's been a long time I haven't seen them, Milton must have took them back. How do you like that, giving a gift and then taking it away. That's terrible manners. It don't surprise me none, though, coming from him.

So I asked the nurse at the desk for candles. —Maime, you asked already for candles. I told you, you can't light candles in your room. We have them in the sanctuary.

She won't give me no candles and even during the war when we were hiding the Polish man there gave us candles. Such an anti-Semite this nurse. The candles what they have in the sanctuary are electricity.

❀ ❀ ❀

While we ate dinner the candles were always in the middle of the table. It was such a good dinner, my mother was cooking for two days. Soup, fish, always a chicken.

First my father says the Kiddush and then he gave a brocha to all the children. To my brother —Gott should make you like Ephraim and Menashe. Then to me and my sister —Gott should make you strong women like Surah, Rivka, Rachel, and Leah. His hand on my hair. —May Gott watch over you in kindness and grant you a life of good health, happiness, and peace.

12

When I was ten years old, the year after my grandfather died, my sister went to America. She was engaged to a man to be married and he wanted to go to America, he was afraid they will get him to fight in the war. It was then the First World War and all the people were afraid.

I remember how the soldiers was coming through the village. The parents had such a hard time with the girls. The soldiers wanted, you know, to have them and they was coming to the houses. My mother would push me to the closet behind the clothes. —Maimela, you're so young, a child only, you don't know what they can do to you. I was staying there until they left the village and outside I hear them shouting to my father —Do you have any daughters? and he says —No, I have only boys. In the closet it was hot and stuffy and smelled like boots.

My mother said it's better for my sister she should go away. I know it must be hard for her but she never showed it, she never said Lia should stay in Poland. She gave my sister some names, addresses of people what she knew from when she came to this country. —Go to them, they'll help you to get started, she said.

Lia packed a trunk with clothes, sheets, things she will need in America. I'm sitting on the bed watching her pack. —Lia, can I come with you to America?

—When you are sixteen you can come. I'll send for you.

—Why not now? I want to go with you now.

—Not now. We don't have yet a place in America. You have to go to school.

—Please, Lia, I won't be a bother. I'll help you. I can cook, you know I can cook.

—No, you stay here and take care of Momma and Tate. They need you here. When you're bigger I will send for you.

Without my sister and my grandfather the house was big and empty. It was strange to wake up in the morning and have the cold place next to me in the bed and in the kitchen the bench without my grandfather's shadow. The chairs at the table was now four, my mother moved the other two back in the corners. So it was me and my brother facing across each other and our parents at the ends. But this was only for a short while. Then there was the accident.

It was an accident with the wagon. My brother was a good driver, my father taught him to handle good the horses, and he would take the wagon to the other village to visit people or to the town to get something what my mother needed. One day a week he was going to see is there any news from America.

MARISA KANTOR STARK

Maybe there will be a letter. Lia didn't write much but once in a while there's something and always my mother is anxious to check. After Lia's first baby was born I remember she sent a photograph and my mother put it on the table. —My first grandchild, she said. —Im y'irtze Hashem there should be many more. And she looked to me and smiled.

Well, on that day I wanted to go with my brother to town but he said —No, I'm in a hurry, if I take you I'll never get home. Because if I was going so I'd see people and talk to people. I tried to make him bring me but he wasn't listening. It was always that way, I wanted him to take me places and he had a reason to say no.

When he came back I was outside by the road, emptying the water from the bucket, and I watched the wagon come closer. I wanted to see was there a letter so I can run first to the store and tell my mother. So I saw the bird, one of those big black birds, how it flew out in front of the horse. It was the kind of bird what Anyushka was afraid from, she said it's bad luck especially if it's crowing, and this one was making a lot of noise. The horse gets frightened, he starts to run faster. My brother shouts to him to stop but he only goes faster and my brother's hand gets tangled in the leather, and he can't stop him. The wagon tips, there is the sound of breaking wood.

I stood there watching, I didn't know what to do. It was all so fast. The wagon broke in two pieces, my brother with the front piece falling over and over. I heard a scream, is that me or is it my brother, and then suddenly there was people, the neighbors and my father all standing around, and the horse was stopped and some blood coming from his head. It was a piece of wood from the wagon what hit him and made him to stop. His dark eyes rolled back in his head, an ugly sound coming from his nose.

There was the wagon in two pieces and my brother lying underneath. —Certainly he's not alive, the people were saying. —It cannot be he is alive.

My father called to him —Motti, Mottel, and pulled away the wagon. I was afraid to look, to see my brother crushed there underneath, but I couldn't turn my eyes away. Then I saw his leg moving slowly, slowly, and he crawled out. My father grabbed him. —It's a miracle from Gott, he held on to him and everyone is saying it's a miracle how Gott made that piece of wood to stop the horse. My brother was very pale and he needed my father to help him walk. But we were thinking it's all right now, everything will be all right, and the neighbors were moving away, going to their business, it was just another thing in all the things what made our life in the village. So people will talk, —Did you hear what was with Motti, Yes, I was there, I saw it, and that will be all.

But that's not how it happened. It was some weeks and still my brother's hand was hurting him. It was the right hand what was wrapped in the leather when he was falling and now there was no strength in that hand. I can feel when he takes my hand how it's very weak and always he was so strong. His hand was getting thinner and thinner until it was only a bone with a little bit skin. There was a hole with pieces of bone coming out and around it was green. I never saw a skin like that color, it was awful to look at.

My mother brought him to the hospital for an operation. Not in the town, she wasn't trusting to the doctor there, to Cracow she took him where there was a hospital. But they said —You should have come before, now we have to cut off the hand. My brother was terribly sick and they cut it off but even still he wasn't getting no better. For many days my mother was with him in Cracow and I was making the meals for my father. We were sitting together at the table but there wasn't too much to say and my father would look at his books and I ate fast and then washed up the plates. I didn't ask what is happening in Cracow.

Then one day she came home and it was only her what came. —Your brother is dead, they told me. They hanged sheets to cover the mirrors.

We was sitting shiva there at the house. The rabbi came with a knife and he cut a piece on my parents' clothes and also on my blouse he cut it and all week we had to wear these clothes. People were coming, bringing fruits and trays of food what was spread out on the table. —Only fifteen years old, they say. —Gott loves him very much, he takes him to spare him the sorrow in this world. My father was talking to them about my brother, that he helped the kittens be born and was growing up to be a doctor. But my mother would not talk. She moved inside herself, if I tried to touch her it was like touching a stone. She sat on a low chair close to the floor, staring down at her lap, tracing with her finger the curving black pattern on her dress. I did not like to go near her. I know I'm only reminding to her about my brother.

My father brought her a plate with some little bit of food she should eat. She pushed it away. He was bending over her chair, his back was to me and he didn't know I was there.

—Ruth, try to be strong. It's a very great sorrow we have, but you can't stop living.

—You can't know, Itzak, how tired I am. I lost two children. I just don't have the strength any more.

—Gott will give you strength, Ruthie. You have still another daughter.

I hear this, I feel a heaviness inside me, tugging at my heart. I am just one person. I know I can never be to them what three children was.

Later my mother started talking again, working in the store, but she was slower and she looked to me smaller, shriveled. She was never the same after my brother died. It was the beginning of her getting old.

All these years I'm wondering what it would be if Motti was not killed in that accident, if he was alive during the war. Would he do different by my parents. I don't know. He was always a good son to them.

13

Three Pesachs we were hiding underground. It wasn't easy and it was easy according as it was. There was no kosher dishes, no nothing. I kashured the stove and they have what they grind flour with, so I made matzohs from the flour and water. We ate potatoes. I had two pots, one for potatoes and one for borscht, and I made borscht from the sourgrass.

Sometimes at night I was making bread. So I tell the man —Get me some yeast, and he was bringing it to me, then I maked bread for us and for him and his wife. Once he left that bread on the table and some neighbors were seeing it. They asked him —Where did you get such a nice bread? and he don't know what to answer. He says —Marina made it. —Oh? When did she get to be such a baker?

Because Marina was his wife and she maked bread like a stone. The Gentiles, they think to put one cup yeast to one pound flour but I know it's better two cups and then the bread is taller, nice and full with holes. It grew so big it don't fit to the oven and my husband had to turn it, it should fit. The stove wasn't like here the stove, it was very deep and you have to reach in to put the bread. My arms aren't long enough.

So I know they're asking about the bread and I told him —You can't leave it anymore where they will see it. I'm making sure he don't leave it.

Marina was many years older than him, she was a widow, forty-four or forty-five, and I don't think he can be more than thirty. He was always talking to her she shouldn't tell people what we were hiding, he was afraid she will forget. Because she was a stupid woman, she don't think at all. She meant well, you understand, only terribly stupid. She wasn't very tidy neither, such clothes she had, like a potato sack, and hair like string down her back. He married her for her property, I'm sure. She had a small piece of land from her first husband.

They had a child, a five-year-old daughter Onyella. We were hiding that she shouldn't see us, a child can't keep quiet, but once she saw us. She was picking sourgrass and she says to a neighbor's child —By us is a Herr and Frau and they cook borscht out of this. The child told her mother and after the war the woman said to me —I knew it all the time you were hiding there. I would have brought you some bread but I was afraid what could happen.

So that's how we was hiding by a man all those months and the neighbor knew and didn't say nothing. It was a miracle from Gott.

The money I gave him I had from before the war, I was saving small bills from the store. Five hundred American dollars, in Europe that was an awful lot of money. Not everybody had but we had. If a man came to the store and he wanted something, let's say tobacco, I said I can get it for you but I want American money. And I put it away. If not for that money we wouldn't live.

When the war came I hid the money under the stoop. There was a loose board on the steps, it was three steps and this was the bottom one, and I took it up and scraped in the dirt not too deep and there I put the money. I told my husband —If I should survive, if you should survive, this is where it will be.

So we were hiding, I say to him —Go back and get that money. It was late at night, twelve or one o'clock, no, between one and two o'clock, nobody should see him. I was so afraid. I was sitting up, praying to Gott he'll find the money and come back to us. Because I know if they was to find him they'll find us where we are hiding. They won't kill him, first they'll hit him and beat him to tell where we are hiding. Then they will kill him. And come for us.

I was waiting. It wasn't so far, maybe half an hour if you're going straight, but I know he can't be going straight he has to take the way around in the fields. I was thinking it's almost two hours, if he don't come in another ten minutes I will have to do something. But what can I do. So I sit and wait.

Then I hear the scraping on the door over our head and I know it is him. We maked a sign he will scrape like that three times and when I hear him my legs go weak, I know now it's all right, at least he's alive. I push up the door. —Saul, did you find it?

—Yes, it was like you said. I reached in my hand and it was there.

We gave the money to the Polish man and I told him where to change it. But only small bills I was giving him because it was during the Second World War and he was a poor farmer, people will be asking where he gets such American money. Then he was taking it to another village to buy food. I told him —Go to a different village, people won't know you and what you're buying. He bought corn, I should make the bread.

My husband don't want me giving him so much money. —You give too much, he doesn't need this much to buy food. He's a shikkur, don't you know he's spending it at the taverns? It's dangerous, when they're drunk they talk.

—He won't talk about us, he's risking his life. I want him to have this money, it doesn't matter to me how he spends it.

—You're crazy, Maime. We'll need it. After the war we'll need money and he's wasting it away.

—It's my money. I thought to hide it. Don't tell me what to do with it.

—I'm saying you are crazy.

When the war was over I wanted we should give him everything, all the bills we had left, but my husband did not want. He was a stingy man, my husband.

—He's a shikkur.

—He saved our life. When we come to America, you wait, I'm going to send him money.

We were terribly sick. All of us had typhus and I had to take care of them. But also I was very sick, I had headaches and a rash on my face and arms and there was the nightmares. I woke up my skin was hot and prickly and I thought there was

MARISA KANTOR STARK

lice crawling over me in the dark. The first time I called out, but this was terribly dangerous if they should hear us, so after that when I go to sleep I put a rag in my mouth, I shouldn't make no noise. My husband and Leibish too, I stuffed their mouths with a rag, because Leibish used to cry and sometimes scream in his sleep. I soaked it with warm water or milk they should suck on it and not throw it away.

All the time I'm thinking what if we still had our parents with us. We could not take care of them. My father-in-law coughing that terrible cough, my mother the way she was. No, with our parents we would never have survived. If not for that what we did, I wouldn't be here even now.

14

He left me here.

—Tanta, you need to be where there are nurses, a doctor. I found you a very nice place. It's close by, right on the outskirts of Newark, and it's kosher.

This was after the operations. I had two, three operations while I was staying by my nephew. Different things was wrong with me, I was having headaches and there was something in my breast it shouldn't spread. I couldn't stay no more at his house. There are stairs, maybe I'll fall and hurt myself.

They put me in the hospital, they gave me all kinds of medicines. Little white pills, the doctor would come with a glass of water, and some bigger ones, a plastic capsule with grains inside like colored sand. That one I couldn't swallow, it made me choke to be eating plastic, so they gave it to me on a spoon with pink applesauce. I hated the applesauce, it had lumps in it, and I never knew which lumps was the apples, which was the pill. But now I don't take it no more, only the white ones what they bring me here.

—It's Edgewood Manor, Tanta. You remember. I wanted Uncle Saul to go there when he was sick. You'll like it, it's a lot of Jewish people.

I don't know when it was. I have no way to keep time, no idea except it was winter. Because I remember it was snowing, very small fine flakes like powder on his hair and sleeve and his brown suede glove holding tight the handle of my suitcase. Our footsteps left prints on the cement walk, what covered up behind us as we came to the sliding glass doors of the building.

Edgewood. I know what that means. It's not that there's so much trees here.

—Of course you know we'll visit you. I'll come, sometimes Debbie, sometimes the children. It'll be almost like when you had your own apartment.

The door is sliding shut. I stand and look out through the glass.

This is false what he was saying. The children don't come.

15

I don't look to be ninety. People say I look young, they're anxious to know my age. And they're not believing me that I'm past ninety.

Looking in the mirror I don't have no wrinkles, only some wrinkles here around the eyes, I don't know can you see them. Because I was very careful, always taking care of my skin. I used to rub butter on my face before I went to sleep.

When I was a girl I had those spots on my face and on my back and I was thinking people are always staring at them. I was very pretty but I can't help this how I was thinking. So I told my mother —I want to take them off.

—No, Maimela, you don't need to change your face.

—They're ugly, Momma. Look at them.

—They're not ugly. This is how you're made.

—But they hurt.

—I don't think they hurt. You always had them, they never hurt you.

—I hate them.

—Stop it, I don't want to hear any more. You're such a pretty girl.

But I wasn't happy. Then one time I was going to the town to a doctor and he took them off. Tzzz. He used a match and burned them, it hurt but I didn't say nothing, I didn't make a sound. I wasn't telling my mother before I went because I know she won't like it. But when I come home I went to her.
—Momma, what's different?

Of course, right away she knew. —Oh, Maimela, you did it. I told you not to.

—I know, but I wanted, it's my face. Don't you see how nice it looks?

She touched my face and it was smooth. —Did it hurt very much?

—No, Momma, it didn't hurt.

—Well, it looks all right. You're a pretty girl. Still I wish you didn't do it. There was nothing wrong with the face Gott gave you.

My hair would be white now but they color it for me red like it used to be. They keep it very short and one time each week the lady comes to comb it and spray it. Then I don't do nothing, I just pat it in the morning like this with my hand. It's very stiff, it don't get messed up even when I'm sleeping. Because I can't be bothered no more to comb it.

I wear lipstick. I always like a bit of lipstick, you know, for some color. Not too dark, not a red like they're wearing it, just this soft pink. I have one what I like, I don't remember now what it's called. Satin something, my nephew brought it. He said his wife Debbie picked it. I don't know but it's not too bad. And sometimes Karyn will make my nails. She comes to say good night, give me a hug and ask if I want something. —Maybe tonight I'll paint your nails? I have a new color, peach. Because she has very long nails and they're always a color. Sometimes more than one color, last week she had white with different kinds of lines across, pink, orange, green, but she took it off because she said she don't like the white, it's too bright and her skin is dark. Well, I don't have nails like that. All the years I was working with my hands, who can keep such fancy nails. But I let her paint them. It makes me feel special like I'm going to a party or what. She has some little balls of cotton and she holds my hand in her hand very still. And all the time my nails are polished I'm very careful, I touch things very gently. Because my hands are looking graceful, I try to move them gracefully.

One time each year I go to the doctor, he should take the wax from my ears. The ear, nose, and throat man. My nephew comes, he's taking me in his car. It used to be I would clean the wax myself with a Q-tip when I washed in the morning but then Karyn saw the Q-tips at the sink and she says —You can't be using these. Would you believe, like I'm a little child. I'm not a child, I can have my Q-tips, but she took them away. So now I go to the doctor.

Once he says —While you're here, maybe you want me to check your hearing. I say —Why not, my hearing is always good and I'm not in no hurry. So he took me into a little room

MARISA KANTOR STARK

behind there, what it was very hot, and he told me put my head down on the table. Then he was banging something on the table. —Yes, I hear it, what do you think, I'm not deaf.

Afterwards when I was going home in my left ear I can't hear so good. My nephew was talking and I don't know what's he saying. But always my hearing was good. I told the nurse at the desk —I go to the doctor and now suddenly I can't hear. So they got me a hearing aid.

But with the hearing aid I don't hear nothing and I went back to the doctor. He says —Look at that, they put it in the wrong ear. He wanted I should come back, they'll fix me for another ear, but it costs a hundred and seven dollars. That's an awful lot of money. My nephew what he pays the bills says it's not so much but he don't fool me, I know what it is.

—Tanta, I want you to get the hearing aid. The doctor says you need it.

—I don't need. It's a lot of money.

—The money's not an issue.

—To me it's an issue.

—I told you not to worry about it. I'll make you an appointment for Tuesday morning, how does that sound?

—No. I have things to do Tuesday.

—What could you have . . . Wednesday, then.

—No.

—Tanta, for once stop being so stubborn.

—I'm a grown woman, Milton. I will decide do I need a hearing aid. And for a hundred seven dollars I don't need.

He handles all the money. I'm getting a pension from the Germans and also my social security, it's all coming to him. I think the pension is more than the social security. You know, for ten years I had a sick husband, I can't be thinking about

money. I gave them they should mail it to Milton, my checks and my husband's checks. My husband told me not to do it.
—What do you want to give him for? It's our money.

—He said he'll take care of it for us.

—Maime, I'm telling you. You give him money, one day you'll cry for it.

But I don't listen to him, I signed it to my nephew. Now he pays for everything. Here it costs an awful lot of money, I didn't know but some people was telling me. He pays the bill. So I thought he'd be helping me, he'll do the checks and such, but I didn't know I will never see the money. Is this right, I shouldn't see my own money. I owe somebody twenty dollars, a friend of mine what was picking up some things for me, a carton of milk and such, a long time ago before I came here. But I don't have with what to pay her. I don't have even a quarter in my change purse.

My mother was saying a person with no money it is like he is dead because he can't go away or do nothing.

MARISA KANTOR STARK

16

This is my day: In the morning after I'm dressed I get washed and then I take my purse with my things in it, what I'll need for the day. There's a tissue and a candy for my throat and some letters what some people was sending me. What else, oh, my glasses for reading, if I want a book from the library at the other side of the building. They have a nice library, it's small but it has shelves and a carpet and some chairs with lamps for reading. I like to read but only when I find a book what's not too long because my memory is not what it used to be. I can't read no more a long book. My eyes get tired and I'm dizzy, I have to stop, and then when my nephew comes he says something.

—Hey, Tanta, caught you napping.

—I'm not sleeping, Milton. I'm resting my eyes.

—I know, I know. So what were those little snoring noises I heard coming from your chair?

He winks at me and I get angry. —Don't you tell me if I'm

sleeping, I know when I'm sleeping. I wasn't sleeping, I was resting my eyes.

—Well, maybe you shouldn't rest your eyes so long. That's why you don't sleep at night.

Of course that isn't why. I have other things at night I'm thinking. But I can't say this to him.

When I pick up the book again I can't remember what it's about. This is very frustrating, how a person can read all those pages and not remember nothing. I used to read very big books, in our house there was a little alcove I was sitting to read for hours. But now I take a shorter book or a magazine. They have different ones all piled up there, I don't think they throw away even one magazine. Even now it's not winter you can read how to make a good winter soup. It has something in it, they say dumplings, but to me they look like kneidlach. I used to make them and they was perfect, big but very light, they float to the top of the soup. I don't cook no more. But the pictures are good, shiny and a lot of color. Sometimes I bring it out from the library to read it here.

I can't sit too much in one place. I have to watch for Herman. He recognizes me from the apartment, they was on the third floor and I was on the second. So he follows after me everywhere, grabbing hold my sleeve, asking —Maime, where is Lou, when are we going to eat? He's always hungry, always looking for food. I see him coming I run the other way, move quickly around the corner he shouldn't find me. I'm always keeping my eyes around me, he shouldn't come up unexpected.

There is one thing, though. I always come out, I don't like to stay in my room. Some people, they wear their slippers all day and their dressing gown and they don't go out at all.

MARISA KANTOR STARK

Lillian does that sometimes, I don't see her at lunch and I know she's in her room still with her rabbit slippers ordering a tray. She tells them she's too tired. But that's not for me. Even if I'm feeling weak I get up and I come here. I don't stay in the room, I'm not that kind. I never order a tray.

When I sit here in my chair so I see people, I talk to people. Sometimes I talk to Lillian. But that's hard, she's deaf and she makes me tired. If I talk to her I have to shout and still she's not hearing what I say.

—How you're feeling today, Lillian?

—I'm waiting for my son. I had a call he was coming.

—That's very nice. What time he's coming?

—What? Oh, in Philadelphia. He lives in Philadelphia. It's a long drive, that's why I don't know exactly when he's coming. I'm waiting for him now.

I always had lots of people. Gott is good to me, wherever I was I always find friends and I always make friends. This is important for people what are coming from another country. The people here don't know me so much but still I'm making friends.

Berta comes by with her walker. She can't walk good, her legs are swollen like a sausage inside her stockings and her knees are big and wrinkled and her ankles drop down over the top of her shoes. She goes very slow, pushing the walker, not picking her feet from the ground. When she sees me she stops and we talk a little bit what's happening. This one is yelling again at the nurses, this one has a visitor.

—Oh, look at the nice flower arrangement they put here.

—Yes, it must be someone had a wedding or a bar mitzvah and was bringing them.

—Are they real?

—I don't know.

—Touch them, Maime, see if they're real.

Berta is only seventy. We had a party with cupcakes and candles for her birthday. There was a clown, a lady with white paint on her face and a little flower painted on her cheek. She was going around, making balloons shaped like different kinds of animals. She came to me where I'm sitting.

—Dog or giraffe?

—What?

—Do you want a dog or a giraffe?

—Can you make an elephant? I think I should prefer to have an elephant.

Some people was saying —What is this, a clown, this isn't a children's party, but I tell the lady —Don't pay no attention to them, they complain about everything, that's just their way. So she maked for me a blue elephant.

Seventy is young. When I was seventy I was living in my own apartment.

If there's something the nurses will tell me —Maime, it's bingo or arts and crafts, and then I go. They have to tell me because I don't have a watch, the part with the numbers is missing and it's just the glass. I wear it anyway, I always wore a watch, but when I look at it only the skin from my arm shows through and I don't know the time or else they tell me or I notice on the clock in the dayroom.

Bingo is two o'clock, that's nice, something to do. It uses time and besides we win things. Berta always wins. She's quick, always the first to hear the numbers how they're calling them. It's because she used to be an accountant. She's not like me, she grew up in this country and she was studying at a university. Here they have so many chances, in Poland it's not like that. So she has a gold necklace and turtle earrings what she won, not real gold, but who would know. It looks the same.

Some people are jealous, they say little remarks, but I'm happy for her that she wins. I told them —Don't you talk that way about my friend, she wins because she deserves to win. Then once I heard a woman say —I'll talk what I want to talk, I don't have to listen to Maime. Do you notice lately how her mind is going? I was terribly angry, I was thinking to hit her with my bag, and that will tell you something because I never hit nobody before, I'm not a violent person. But I didn't hit her, it's not how I'm raised. I said —There's nothing wrong with my mind, thank you. And my heart neither, what I'm sorry I can't say the same for you. She gave me a nasty look but I didn't stay and after that I don't talk to her no more. If I pass her in the hall maybe I nod and she makes like she don't see me.

A few times I win at bingo. Last week I won some greeting cards, I didn't realize but Berta was telling me. —Maime, look at your card, you have bingo.

—Where?

—There, look, diagonal. She just called G-14.

—You're sure? I didn't hear.

—Of course I'm sure. Nurse, look Maime has bingo.

—Yes, I have a bingo. See, right here, diagonal.

The greeting cards are very pretty but I'm not having what to send them. I can't write because my hand is shaking and anyway who would I send a card. So I put them here in my purse and sometimes I take them out and look at them. Like this one, it has a lamp and it says Happy Birthday and then you open it, Just a shade late. A shade late, what's that supposed to mean. They write the strangest things. Well, whatever, they're pretty cards. So I'm keeping them.

❀   ❀   ❀

What they have each day is written up there on the blackboard by the door of the dayroom, every day a different thing. Bingos is Tuesday, it used to be Friday but now Friday is the exercises. Only they don't call it exercise they say sitter-cise because the people are sitting. You know, they're not all like me, some of them are in wheelchairs or like Berta they have a walker or sometimes a cane. So then that lady with the blond hair and the big silver earrings made like music notes comes with her tape machine. She plugs it in over there by the side. —Arms up, up reach for the ceiling. Good, reach reach reach. Now lower. Hands on your lap. Relax. Gooood. Let's try it again. Reach . . .

She has clothes like you wouldn't believe, skinny black pants what to me look like stockings. I was thinking she should have a skirt over them and I told Karyn once —That lady is missing her skirt, but she laughed and said —Those are leggings, Maime, you don't wear no skirt with them. Still, I don't see how she can come out that way to a place without nothing to cover her.

I don't like the music what she plays. It's too fast, I can't understand the words, so to me it's just noise not music. Also I feel silly waving my arms like that. Mostly it don't matter none, we're all doing it together, but I don't like it somebody else should see me. Like once my nephew was come during these exercises and I saw him through the glass of the dayroom

MARISA KANTOR STARK

so I stopped doing it. The lady said —Don't stop, Maime, you can't be tired already, reach, reach. But I said —No, I'm sorry, I have to go now, and I go out to my nephew.

—Tanta, I hope I didn't interrupt something important. I hear there's music going in there.

—No, it's nothing important.

—What were you doing, I don't want to take you away. How about if I join you?

—No, no. Really, they're not doing nothing. It's just some music they're playing.

Wednesday is color day. Every week we're supposed to have a different color, this week I see it will be red. Well, if I forget to check the board so then I don't know to be wearing it. Last time it was green and I wore this dress with the flowers. Some people was saying —Maime, it's green day, what are you wearing that dress? But I have only this one clothes, what can I do. I was a little bit depressed I wasn't wearing green. The others all had green, Berta had a very nice purple and green dress with a belt and a white collar.

I like arts and crafts the best. I like to make things. When I was a little girl I used to make some nice dolls. Now it's hard for me, but once I maked a hat. Yes, a hat, well, the hat by itself I didn't make. The lady was giving it to us, a straw hat, but it was just plain and we had to decorate it. There was things on the table there to use, ribbons, feathers, some pretty beads.

I took the glue and put a little dot very careful like she says —Just a little dot, you don't need so much glue. Then I picked a bead, first a blue bead, then a red, then another blue all the way around. Now some green feathers, there that looks very nice.

I see Herman is trying to eat the glue.

—No, Herman this is not food, this is glue. You can't eat it.

—I'm hungry, when can I eat?

—Soon. Look at the nice hat what I'm making. You want I should help you make a hat?

—Where's Lou?

—She's coming, later you will see her. Do you want to make for her a hat? A nice . . . no, no, you can't eat that, it's not food. It will make you sick.

I try to help people, I'm a good person. If you talk to people they will tell you I help people, sick people, and I feed people. In the evening before the news I go around, I help the nurses to feed people what can't do for themselves, can't come to the tables for dinner.

And I stop the fights and things. Yesterday afternoon there was a lady playing songs on a guitar and one woman in her wheelchair was shouting —Help me, and swinging her arms around. Then another woman yells to her —Shut up, what's your problem, can't you appreciate some good music? but she kept doing it so I wheeled the chair out into the hall. She asked me —Do you have a dollar, one dollar in your pocket? and I patted her shoulder. —Here, you'll be all right.

Because I was always giving tzedakah, dealing with people so Gott should deal with me. This is how I am. I'm a good person. What I can do, I do.

But one day Milton was come and sitting in a corner, not telling me he is here. When he saw me feeding the people he smiled, nodded his head. He didn't say nothing but I know what he's thinking. He's like one of those people who does

MARISA KANTOR STARK

only for himself. I think he's never done nothing for people a day in his life except he's getting something from it.

He's not my nephew really, he's my husband's nephew. His father was my husband's older brother what came to America after the First World War. He passed away very quickly and also his wife. They were sick with something, I think scarlet fever. So Milton grew up like an orphan, living sometimes with this relative, sometimes with that one. But later, after I came to this country, he always said I am his favorite aunt. Because I was giving him things. He used to come to the apartment, I maked him cakes. I kept them in the oven on trays and he would go straight to the oven and look inside for the cakes. —Walnut, my favorite. Tanta, I always say you're the best baker in the world.

—You're like a little child, I said, —always wanting sweets. But I was pleased.

Then later with my pension and my social security, I gave over everything. Everything what I had in the bank now it's under his name. I didn't expect he's going to handle me like this.

My husband warned me.

17

I got married when I was very young. Sixteen I was engaged. My husband Saul was from another village. He was my cousin. Well, not really my cousin, my grandfather and his grandfather was cousins. He was five years older.

When we were very young our fathers was agreeing we should be married together. —We know each other, you know the family, they said. —You know what to expect. This is not really true, you don't know nothing, but that's how they were saying.

So they were come to the house I should meet them. I cannot be more than eight years old, and my father was introducing us. —Maime, this is Saul and his parents. He looks just like all the other boys but very dark and tall, I'm not even up to his chest. I give him my hand like my mother says but his palm is hot and wet and I let go to wipe my hand on my coat. —Such a scrawny little thing, his mother said. —So many freckles.

I stare at her. She has a very big nose, too big for her face. My brother told me that's because people when they get older their nose keeps growing even the rest of them does not. He said only if every day you will stroke the nose like this on the side it keeps it from growing. I wasn't sure to believe him or not but it can't hurt, so for every night before I went to sleep I was stroking my nose, just in case, it shouldn't get big like Saul's mother. Just the other day I remember this and I looked in the mirror to see now I am old do I have a big nose like what she had. But no, my nose isn't so big, I checked from all the sides. Maybe my brother was right and it was good I listened to him.

So it was we were growing up and sometimes Saul was coming with his parents to the house. Not often, it wasn't so close, but once in a while they came and sat, his parents and my parents together in the house, while we were outside playing. My mother would serve something, some cake, and she'd call us in to sit there by the adults. Outside we was loud but when we come in we sat quiet and not looking to one another.

Saul used to tease me and pull at my braids. —Maime, Maime, come play catch with us. Him and my brother had an egg, you know, from our chickens, and they said —Don't worry, it's a cooked egg, see if you can catch it. So I caught it and it broke all over my hands and my dress, such a mess I was making, and they laughed and ran together away to the barn.

His father was an egg candler. He would take the egg and hold it up by the candle to see maybe it has some kind of spot, maybe some blood. So my husband was learning this trade from his father, like his father learned it from his father when he was young. They was not a learned family. Very religious, but not learned. My husband didn't go too much to school, he left school so he could learn the trade. But he didn't like it, there wasn't a lot of money in the egg business. He started something else, dealing in lumber, and this was a very good business. He was a very good businessman, my husband.

When we got older for a while I don't see him too much because I was going to school and I'm with my friends. A lot of times during the week I stayed in the village by the school. I stayed by a family, I shouldn't have to walk back alone in the dark, and my mother was paying for me to stay there. She gave me food for the entire week, bread, butter, cheese to give to the family, and then on Shabbos I was coming home.

But when I finished school I started to work with my mother in the store and then once a week he would come. Sometimes alone, sometimes with another man what they were partners, and he came to the house or to the grocery where I was working. He was very good-looking. Such dark eyes. My mother would see him through the window and she said to me —Go with him, Maimela, I can take care of it here.

So we were walking in the village and he talked about his business. Always about the business. He was very excited about it, the money he will make. —I can see already, Maime, how it's going to be. They'll need more and more wood for the train tracks, it will be a very big business. And the money from that business, I'll invest it to buy horses. There's a lot of money in horses. When we're married you won't need anymore to have a store.

He was taking my arm. Such a good-looking man, dark and tall. And I am light. They say we are a nice couple. —Maime, he's so good-looking. Someday he will be rich.

My father was asking me. —You like him, Maimela?

—I like him.

—Because he's from a good family, a relative. And he's a smart man. I think you'll be happy.

He only wanted I should be happy.

18

The wedding my parents maked at the house. We had a big house and my mother and Anyushka was cooking and baking for days. It was good to watch my mother getting ready these preparations. More and more now I would see her standing around like she can't think what she is or what to do. This my mother who was always busy and sure of things all the years I'm growing up. I tried to hide this from myself, pretend it's not this way. My mother is what I'm looking to be strong. But behind me I knew it was there.

One day I came into the store she was standing staring out the window at the rain and the pools of mud in the yard. There was a woman in the back of the store, looking for something on the shelf.

—Look at those puddles, Maimela.

—I know, all day it was raining. What are you doing, Momma?

—Nothing. It's raining, there's nothing to do.

—There's a customer. In the back.

—Oh yes, it's Faige. I don't know what she's looking for.

—Well, why don't you ask her?

She sighed. —I will. I'm just going.

She moved past me. Her face came very close and when I looked at it, I saw suddenly it was not familiar to me. Always my mother's face was like looking to a mirror, people was saying we look like sisters. But now this was something different, the face of an old woman I don't know. There was shadows under her eyes and lines like threads around her mouth.

I was sad, the kind of sadness what leaves you feeling empty and cold. My mother was gone from me. But then the sadness was changed to anger. It didn't have to be this way. What was she doing, just standing there when there was a customer. Did she forget how to run a grocery. I wanted to grab her and shake her, tell her to stop behaving this nonsense. I left quickly the store.

From all my friends I was married first. We were still young, they were still meeting people. Well, now I know that way is better but then I was thinking why should I wait, he has a good business. I was the youngest, my friends at that time was all three, four years older, and when I looked at the girls my same age I thought they are like children, they don't know nothing about men. But it was me didn't know. I was going for the good looks. I felt something here in my heart but I should know that don't mean nothing, it don't mean you will be happy.

When I told Raisa I was getting married she couldn't believe. —Married already? Maime, what's the hurry, you're so young.

—I love him.

—Do you really? How can you tell, you hardly know him.

—What do you mean, I don't know him? We grew up together, he's part of the family.

—Yes, but what kind of man is he? I mean he's very good-looking but what else?

—What are you trying to say, Raisa? You're telling me I shouldn't marry him?

—I didn't say that.

—You're jealous, maybe?

—No.

—I think yes. I think because you're three years older and you're not engaged even.

—Forget about it, Maime. Forget I even said anything.

But it comes out she was right, I was too young. Other people were also saying. They heard I was getting married and they was asking my father —She's so little, did she finish school yet? I didn't hear them but one night I heard him talking to my mother when he thought I wasn't listening. So I know what they were saying.

When the girls were getting married first they were inviting everyone, the whole families. Like Raisa's sister was married and I was going to the wedding and all my family was going. But then it got too much, too many people. So they were doing it modern, inviting only the youngsters, the girl's friends. Well, some older people, some relatives, but mostly the younger people. They came from the other villages.

I had my mother's wedding dress what she fixed to me so it would fit. It was a beautiful dress, a cream color, and very simple, not with all those laces and ruffles and such. There was a very fine embroidery at the top with little pearl buttons.

MARISA KANTOR STARK

One of the buttons came loose, it was hanging from a thread, and the day before the wedding my mother sewed it for me. I was kneeling on the floor next to her chair, my hair was tied in rags, and she had the dress on her lap. —This was my mother's dress, your grandmother Maime. She died when I was very young.

—I know.

—But I remember some things about her. I remember her singing to me before I fell asleep, I was very little and sleeping in the bed there with my parents. Sometimes at night I would wake up hot and crying and her hands were cool on my face. She would sing to me softly in Jewish, the same songs I sang to you. You're named for her, do you know they also called her Maimela? My father called her that.

She held up the dress. —Well now, that's better. I'll give you my comb with the pearls to have for your hair. It matches perfect the dress. You know, I wanted Lia to wear this dress when she was married.

I don't say nothing. Lia was married in a little shul in New York and I don't have no idea what she wore. Nobody from the family was there.

At some weddings they're dancing separate, the men in one circle the women in one circle. But at my wedding we were doing it different. There was a man from the village what plays the fiddle and we danced together, first in a circle then this one dancing with that one, and that's how I like it. We danced for hours, all the afternoon and into the dark, we stopped only for a little time the man should eat. I take off my shoes and dance on the grass with Raisa and then with my husband. They put me on a chair and my husband on a chair and they picked it up to dance around us. So it's tilting this way and that way, they had something, you know, to drink, and I'm holding tight to the chair and laughing.

It was getting late, only a few people are left dancing. The fiddler calls this will be the last dance. I go to my father where he's sitting and watching. —Tate, come dance with me. This last dance.

I wasn't thinking he will say yes, I never seen my father dance. But he got up and took my hand. His hand on my waist, he swung me around.

—Tate, you know how to dance!

—I was also young once, Maimela.

He was so strong, I could feel the strength in his hands. I wasn't this close to my father since I was a little girl and he held me in his lap. I tilted my head back, I'm not even as tall as his shoulder, to see his face. He was looking down at me and in the light from the lanterns there is such a love in his eyes. I never saw a love like that. It was like I can see inside him, down through his eyes and into his soul, and for a minute I was frightened. I knew anything in the world he would do for me. And I cannot say why but I was afraid.

MARISA KANTOR STARK

19

After I was married I emptied my things to be moving in with my in-laws. For seven years I lived with them in that house in the other village. It wasn't so easy. The house was very small, there was no place to move they weren't there. My mother-in-law was always saying I should be cleaning this and working that, if I was sitting and reading so she found for me a job. And I was still young, I was growing even. When I came home to visit after two months I was married the people ask my father —Is that Maime, we don't recognize her, she grew up. Because you know, girls can be growing until they are twenty-four.

My mother-in-law wanted I should cut my hair. —Married girls cut their hair, she said, and she gave me a tichel to cover it. It was a scarf such like she was wearing, ugly brown with orange threads and a fringe along the edge. But I won't wear it and I won't cut my hair. I had it in braids crossed on top my head. —No, I like it long.

—For shame, Maime. Other men will look at you.

—I don't care. That's their fault if they look.

—All the years I'm married I have my hair short and covered like this. All good Jewish women do it this way. For you it's not good enough?

—I don't want. My mother didn't cut her hair.

—So, that makes it right? You're not your mother.

—I'm more to my mother than to you. I tell you, without my hair I'd feel like a different person.

—Such mishegas. You'll be the very same person with short hair. I never saw a girl so stubborn.

She told my husband —Maime should cut her hair, but my husband says —This fighting has nothing to do with me, it's for you two to decide. Because he did not get involved between me and my mother-in-law, when there was some argument he pulled back like behind a wall. Not he didn't listen, it was that he didn't hear even, he was deaf. Over the years there was other times he was like this, not hearing nothing what I'm saying. So I learn to go ahead with myself what I have to do. I listen what it says inside me and that is all.

Only later in America, after my parents and my husband's parents was gone, I was finally cutting it. I woke up early one morning and took the knife from the kitchen and one, two I cut off my braids. It was very fast and then I wrapped them in a newspaper and put them away in a drawer. When my husband woke up he saw me and he said —What is this, what did you do to your hair? —What does it look like I did, I cut it. I'm tired of it long.

MARISA KANTOR STARK

He did not like it, he says I'm doing without thinking, I'm always doing without thinking, but what does he know about it. He never knew what it is I'm thinking. So it's done and there's not nothing he can do. I don't know what happened to the braids. When we left that apartment I emptied all the drawers but I didn't find them. It was fine to me that they were gone.

My husband's father Yusef was an older man, much older than my father. He wasn't talking much. All day long he worked as an egg candler driving the cart around to the different farmers. At night after supper he would sit watching the fire, not saying nothing, just sitting, smoking his cigars. His boots were lying by the chair, giant brown work boots, and I thought if I was still a little girl I could curl up and fit myself inside one of those boots. Because he was a big man, like a bear, and when he sat he filled up the chair.

Slowly the room would fill up with the smoke from his cigars. It was a thick tobacco smell, but not unpleasant, when I breathed up deep into my head it made me feel calm and dreaming. His clothes, the heavy shirts what he wore, always smelled like that smoke and I notice my own clothes and even my hair starts to smell that way when I'm lying with it spread onto my pillow. It was a new smell, the smell of my new married life, and I carried it around with me.

My father-in-law sat until the fire burned low. Across from him my mother-in-law was sitting, doing something with her hands. She was always busy, there was a coat what needed to be fixed or a hem. I used to wonder if there's no work will she create some, maybe unravel a hole in a sock so she can fix it. While she worked she talked. She was such a yenta, everything about the neighbors she knew and she was telling my father-in-law. —Do you know, Georg's wife is having twins they think. The doctor was there today and he put his hand on her stomach and said there's two babies kicking inside her. That's why such pains.

I never know how much my father-in-law listened to what she said. I couldn't tell from his face what he was thinking. He had a gray beard down to his chest and a mustache hiding his mouth, this gave him a very stern look. And he had dark eyes, sharp. I was a little bit afraid of him.

But one night he surprised me. It was not long after we was married and my mother-in-law was talking again I should cover my hair. I was at the table, reading a book and making like not to hear. —You shouldn't read so much, she said. —You'll ruin your eyes, Maime, and then your children will have bad eyes.

Then suddenly he says —Gussie, I told you, leave her be. His voice was quiet but there was something in it, a warning underneath, and I looked up quickly. He was staring at my mother-in-law. —Enough. She looked down at her sewing. —All right, all right. I didn't mean anything.

She starts to talk something else and soon after this they're gone to bed, they always go right when the fire burns down and got up very early. My father-in-law didn't say nothing to me. But I don't forget how he spoke up for me. I notice my mother-in-law was easier with me after that and I wasn't afraid of him no more.

Once he brought for me a goat. Because sometimes the farmers where he was working couldn't pay him and they gave

MARISA KANTOR STARK

him potatoes, onions, different things, and one man gave him a goat. He came to me in the yard where I was peeling potatoes and he had the goat on a rope. —Maime. I thought maybe you'd like to have him.

I knew he could sell the goat, that was what the man expected he will do and get the money what was owed him. It was a baby goat, I can see the little horns just starting to grow, he can probably get some good money. But he was standing there, holding out the rope. I took it from him. —Yes, I'd like that. I like animals.

—Good, when I have some time I'll make a hut for him in the yard.

He went inside.

I called the goat Gadya like the one in the Pesach haggadah. It's a song we sing at the end of the seder about the little goat what the father bought for his son and always it was my favorite song from the whole seder. I love the rhyming Aramaic words, the fast melody, how everybody comes with life again after the long night to sing together and bang the rhythm on the table. We used to have very big seders at my house with neighbors and relatives from the other villages around. One of my mother's brothers came with his children, two hours they was riding to us in the wagon, and when the seder is over at midnight they crowded into the rooms to sleep, it's too late for going back. My cousin Bella used to sleep with me, her feet touching to my feet, our heads at the opposite sides of the bed.

At Pesach time they had here what they call a model seder, some people was coming and making it at the tables in the dining room. They had matzohs and the white horseradish what they grind it very fine it makes the inside of your nose burn and the tears come. I waited at the end they should sing chad gadya. So they sang it but it wasn't the same how I remembered. Because they did it slow, people shouldn't lose the words, and it's not meant to be a slow song.

❊   ❊   ❊

That goat followed me everyplace. If I was going somewhere so I had to tie him with a rope he shouldn't follow. He grew bigger and one day my mother-in-law was going outside to bring in the clothes what are drying in the yard and they was all in rags. All the aprons and my father-in-law's shirts were chewed away in great big holes.

—Maime, come out here please. Right now. Just look what that animal of yours did. Don't you feed him, he has to eat our clothes?

—What happened? I know I tied him up.

—Well, it doesn't help anymore to tie him. He chewed through the rope.

—Oh, you bad boy, what are we going to do with you? I'm sorry, Gussie, I think we have to hang the clothes up higher.

—Oh no, that's not it. The clothes I'm hanging how I always hang them. What we have to do is get rid of the goat.

I know this means she'll bring it to the shochet, they will kill it, and I'm sick to think on it. I seen the inside of the barn where he works, the meat hanging on giant hooks and the blood dripping into the sawdust on the floor. The people bring their cows and sheep there. They leave the meat like that for some days until all the blood is drained away and then they take it down and pack it with salt to pull out whatever little bit is left. The shochet has a coat what was stained brown from the blood and his hands and arms up to the elbows also are stained and even his eyes, little eyes sunk into his face, are red like blood. The barn and the air around it smells like blood what I taste on my tongue like metal when I breathe.

Again it was my father-in-law who saved me. That night my mother-in-law told him what happened and how she's thinking to get rid of the goat. —We can get good money from him, like you should have got in the first place, she said. I felt his eyes move to my face. Just for a minute, then he looked away, but in that minute I knew he won't let her to do it.

—No, Gussie, this is Maime's goat. I will make a stronger door for the hut.

—But Yusef . . .

—I said I will make a door.

And the next day there was a new door with a wood bar and after that whenever my mother-in-law was washing she called me to close Gadya in the hut. So that's how it was. All the time I was living there I felt my father-in-law watching out for me.

20

With many things in my life I had mazal but not with my marriage. My husband could not have children. He wasn't feeling nothing, you would think he was healthy. But it was something wrong.

He said it was from me, I should see a doctor. I was young, what did I know from these things, and I was thinking he must be right. So I went to a doctor but he couldn't find nothing, he says —You are healthy. Then I go to other people, big doctors, because, you know, I had plenty of money, this wasn't a problem, and finally one doctor said to me —I have to see your husband. Well, my husband didn't want to go, he says it can't be from the man, but I told him —The doctor said I should bring you. He had a respect for doctors, what they're saying he thinks it must be right. So we went together. The doctor checked me then he checked my husband and he called me to the side. —You can have children with any man but not with your husband. If you want children it will not be from him.

I never knew it can be that way, I thought like my husband, everything children must come from the woman. But that's what he said. So then I knew and my husband knew. It was like a great burden was taken off me but now there's a new one, I will never have my own children to raise. And this was worse because now it's not my fault there is also nothing I can do to change it. I used to think if I do something different, a different time of the month maybe or I lie very still afterwards, then I can make it happen. But now there is nothing, only to accept this is how it will be.

He stopped talking about it. Once his mother said to me —Nu, Maime, so where are the grandchildren? and he said —Quiet, Momma, you don't know what you're saying. It was the only time he spoke up to her about me.

Then we didn't talk about it no more, what was there to say. But always it hanged there between us. For some time it was a sharp pain inside me, then as the years passed it gets duller, another hurt what is just another part of my life. Still it never disappeared and when I see a family with children it will rise up in my heart like a flame. I told myself it isn't his fault he is this way but that don't change things for me. I feel to him in those times something bitter and I look on him like he is a stranger. I wake up at night he's sleeping there in the bed and I turn to my side and watch him, his chest moving up and down, his hands what touched me lying on the blanket. I breathe the sharp smell from his skin. And I think to myself how did it happen I married this man.

I could have got a divorce. Today there are people what they're living separate and such, I know lots of people. Like I know one of Berta's children is divorced and she has children by another husband. Berta was not telling this to nobody but I found out because one time she said her daughter's husband is one thing, I think she said Gerald, and then the next day she was changing it to Todd. So when I asked her she said —Oh, yes, well his name is Gerald Todd, sometimes we call him Todd, sometimes Gerald. I didn't say nothing but I see how it is.

I could have had . . . there was always lots of people. Wherever I go I meet people, I have lots of friends. And there was plenty of men. I remember my girlfriends used to say to me about the milkman's son Yaakov —He likes you, Maime, always driving you in his cart. He was a good boy with a soft voice and very nice manners, I can like such a one. Then after I was married the rabbi what came around to the village, he didn't have yet a wife and he was a very learned man, not like my husband. So maybe I was wrong to stay with him, sometimes I think this was a big mistake. I could have a family and I wouldn't be here like this alone.

I wasn't happy. I was married too young, living with in-laws. I missed my own parents.

If I had grandchildren now I would name them for my parents. My nephew named his third daughter Ruth after my mother. When he told me I was glad but I know it's not right, not how it's meant to be. Because it was me what survived and from me should be the children to give these names. But you see even this I can't do for them.

I can't remember now did Milton name any children for my father.

But he was my husband and I couldn't leave him. If it's right or wrong I don't know but that's how I am. We had our life the way that we had. And what we went through kept us

MARISA KANTOR STARK

always together until the last. It had to be that way. No matter how it was between us there was no one else shared the burden what we shared.

21

You know, Hitler is still alive. They are saying after the war the Germans killed him but he's still alive. You can be changing the face. There are people with a big nose and they make a small nose. So you can be changing the face, it's only the eyes what you can't change. He was young, forty-six, and he had a mustache. You can shave a mustache. Now he won't be so old, maybe seventy.

He was such a Hitler. What he was doing to the Jewish people you have no idea. It was a terrible war. Then after the war he was running away and hiding. They are saying he is killed but he's not killed. He is still alive.

22

In the village where I was living with my in-laws, so my sister-in-law was also living. My husband had one brother and two sisters. One sister was gone to America when she was single but the other one lived near my in-laws, her parents. She was married, she had fourteen children. Can you believe, fourteen, and there was only two bedrooms. They slept all together in one big room, the boys on one side the girls on one side, with a curtain in the middle to separate and the beds lined up all every different ways.

First she had six girls and we're saying —It must be she wants a boy, but then she had a boy and another boy and still she don't stop. She was a very big woman, she had to have loose dresses. When I was seeing her I never know is she pregnant this time or not.

I was helping with those children like they was my own children. I take them for walks, give them things. Also I paid for the rabbi. He was coming to teach the children in the village, six months this child, six months another child, and he used to live with whatever family. My sister-in-law can't afford to be keeping him there, it was a lot of money to feed him and such, so I was paying he should stay there and the children should learn.

They were all killed in the war. The Hitlers took away the children, killed the whole family. Such sweet children. The little boys had long yellow curls, until they was three years old my sister-in-law didn't cut it, the devil should think it was a girl. She tied their hair back away from their face with a ribbon and after it was cut I hardly recognize them, they look so grown-up. All of them have two names, Yehuda Moshe, Nachum Zev, I don't know how she thought of so many names. The girls also. There was one, I think the third one, she had a trouble with her tongue, some kind of a lisp. I was sitting down with her and making her repeat different words how I say them, she should grow up knowing to talk straight.

I always remembered all their names when even my mother-in-law came confused which was who. She would call —Schaindel, get me an onion, and the child says —I'm not Schaindel, I'm Rivkie. —Well, whatever. Go get me an onion. But I knew each child and what they liked. I told them stories and made them sugar candy like I know from my father.

They used to help me in the store. Because from my mother I was learning how to have a store and when I was by my in-laws I maked a grocery. It was close to the house, so close it was touching, and the door opening to the street. It used to be it was a milk-house, the house belonged to my mother-in-law's parents and they was keeping cows, but now for a long time it was empty, and I put shelves and things. My father-in-law helped me. People was coming, mostly Gentile

MARISA KANTOR STARK

people. I had there tobacco for the cigars, in Poland a lot of people like tobacco but not everybody can be having. But I had and they knew I had so they're coming to the store and sometimes they paid me American dollars. Then maybe they buy another something, a little bit of sugar or some flour.

My husband don't want at first I should have this store. —I make a very good business, what do you need a store?

—I want to have my own. I can't sit all the time in this house doing nothing.

—There is plenty to do. You don't need a store.

But I made the store and he got used to it, I made very good. The whole family liked it. I used to bring my father-in-law tobacco, he kept it in a wood box on the shelf over the fireplace and if I notice when it's getting low, so I fill it for him. And my mother-in-law, she wouldn't say but I know she appreciates also to have. She could step from the house and get everything what she needed. When she was making a cake and there isn't enough sugar she would come in and I would give her. Sometimes she stayed around if there wasn't too much customers and we would talk a little bit, she told me what was going on, who was going with who and such like that. After I was gone I think she missed me.

Because I didn't stay there. After some years I left my in-laws to move to the town. My husband had an uncle what had a grocery there in town and this man came to me. —Would you like to be a partner? He heard I made such a good grocery and he himself was not a businessman. On Wednesday when people was coming to him for yeast to make challahs for Shabbos he would tell them —Oh, I'm sorry, I just sold my last yeast. What kind of way is that to have a business, to have no yeast for challahs. So I said —Yes, I will come.

Then I told my husband —I want to move to the town. I'm going to be a partner in this store.

—You have already here a store.

—No, this is a bigger one. I can do better.

—I don't know. We'd have to leave my parents.

—Seven years I've been living with in-laws. It is enough.

—They're my parents, Maime. I don't like to leave them.

—Saul, I'm not living all my life in another woman's house. I already told him yes, I am going. If you want to come, you can come.

The town is different from the villages. The houses there are bigger and there is more of them, and the streets are stone instead of dirt. There is the post office and different stores, not just a grocery. Like there's one tiny shop where a woman sells all kinds of grasses what they use for medicines. She goes out herself to the fields and woods to pick them and she has them in jars and hanging to dry from the ceiling. The shop is dark and smells like the woods after it rains. If you come in you tell her what's wrong, she will give you something. This for the stomach, this for the women. Soak it first in hot water and drink. Women from the villages all around know her, my mother-in-law knows her. She gives me a plant with tiny purple flowers and tells me drink it at night before I go to sleep with my husband, but I tell her —No, I won't take that, because I'm never believing such things.

On the corner is the store what sells wigs for the women. One time soon after we moved to the town the man who owns that store sees me walking and he comes up to me. —Excuse

MARISA KANTOR STARK

me, but you have such nice hair. It's not often I find that color. I'll give you ten ducats for it.

—I'm not cutting it, I say.

—But it will grow back. Ten gold ducats. Think what you can do with the money.

—I don't need the money, thank you. I will keep my hair.

—I have a customer that especially wants red hair. Maybe you'll change your mind?

I can't think what it will be to see another woman walking on the street with my hair. I tell him I'm sorry, it's impossible, my mind is set. But he's not giving up so easy. After that every time I see him he calls to me —Ten ducats! Hair grows very fast, especially in the summer. I just shake my head and keep walking.

My husband built a beautiful house at the edge of the town by the woods. It had nine rooms, bigger than any house I ever lived in, and a big yard with a place in the back for the horses. In the summertime I would go into the woods to pick raspberries, make them into jam. Maybe you don't know, you wouldn't think, but Poland is a very pretty country in the summer. There are flowers and berries, big raspberries such like I never saw in this country. And they are sweet. But it isn't a place for Jewish people.

After some years my in-laws was thinking to come live by us in that house. My mother-in-law wasn't used to it no more without us, to be alone all day, and she don't like it. She says it's nice and quiet now without me slamming the door all the time, because I used to forget and let it shut too quickly, but I can see really she misses me coming in and out from the store. And my father-in-law also, he says to me —The room feels empty at night without you, Maime, there's nothing new to think about. Because I used to read to him from my books and he liked that, he didn't know himself to read but he was very interested, especially in things to do with other places. It doesn't matter what. —My life is very small, he said to me once. —I've never been anywhere. Never seen anything outside of Poland.

To say the truth I missed it too, my in-laws' house. I liked living in the town, it's more people to see, coming from the villages and such, and the house was beautiful. But it was so big and just for me and my husband and the one maid. Sometimes I missed the other house with its tiny rooms and stuffed up spaces. When I'm doing the wash I think of my mother-in-law, how on Tuesday mornings we used to put a wooden board between two chairs for scrubbing and work together, her on one side, me on the other. I never would have thought it, I thought I'll only be happy to have my own place, but it's always that way, hard to leave what is familiar. Even you know you have to leave it, still it's hard. My life was always moving.

My husband said maybe this is a good idea they will come live with us. —They're getting older, Maime, he said. But I was thinking about it and I decide I want to have my own parents. My in-laws were something to me but they was not my parents, and parents and in-laws you can't live together. —Saul, your parents have your sister to watch out for them, she's living nearby with the children. My parents don't have anyone. My sister is gone, my brother's gone, they need me to take care of them.

Because they were such parents to me, giving me everything. It was hard for me to see how old they got in those ten years since I was married and moved away. I won't see them for a while and then I visit and it was a shock, I have to be very careful my face shouldn't show how I'm feeling. My mother

MARISA KANTOR STARK

especially wasn't well. When I take her hands I can feel the bones, thin and light like pencils, and the skin on her cheeks like a fine, white paper. She reminds me from a bird what once died while I held it, a body without weight in my hand.

—Maime, where's Lia? I haven't seen Lia.

—Lia? She's in America, Momma. You know that.

—Yes. Why I never see her?

Her gray eyes are far away and cloudy behind her memories. I don't know how to answer her when she goes like this. I feel gentle to her, like a baby or small animal I'm left to take care of, but at the same time I was uncomfortable to be with her. And I was ashamed to myself feeling that way.

Someday that will be me, I thought. I will be old, where will I be, who will take care of me then? I touched my hands to my own face to feel my skin. My body was not so young like it used to be.

—Be patient with your mother, my father told me. —She can't help it she's like this.

—It must be hard for you, Tate.

—Not so hard, we manage. There is a lot of things she needs me to do for her but I'm glad to do it.

But I watched him and I saw how slow he moved. If he was walking he would sometimes stop, hold on to the chair or the table if he thinks nobody is looking. His knees was always hurting him, even when he was resting, and whenever he sat down he rubbed his hands over them around and around in little circles. How can he take care of her, I ask myself. It was always hard for me to imagine my parents alone together in the house what used to have so many of us. Turning around each other in the empty rooms. So I brought them to me there in the house in town. They lived there with us all the years, until we had to leave. They had their own room on the bottom floor.

I start to know that my parents will die. I ask myself which is better should go first, and it seems to me impossible there should be one of my parents without the other. They are like two trees what their branches are grown together, without the one the other will fall. Then I hear myself thinking who is it I need more, my father or my mother. You are a terrible person to think this way, I say, terribly selfish, and I try to chase it from my mind. But it keeps coming back to me, when I'm lying in bed, when I'm alone working the store. Stop it, stop it, I'm shouting inside. This is nothing in your hands. I had no idea how it would turn out to be.

MARISA KANTOR STARK

23

When they came to the house I remember the dog was crying. He was a big black dog and he was on a chain there in the yard. —Aus, aus! they came with guns, —everybody out! Stamping, shouting, the dog crying. Some things I won't never forget.

The war broke out September 3, 1939. First they was taking just the businesses, making laws the Jews cannot be moving or traveling. My husband used to go to the other towns, to the sawmills to get lumber, and he could not be going now no more. They took away the grocery. They came with trucks and loaded everything away. —The soldiers need, they said. —The Germans can use all this what you have here. Filthy Jews. He spit on the floor.

Some people were leaving, going to Russia. It wasn't hard then to leave, it was just the beginning. So me and my husband were talking to be going.

My father wanted we should go. —Leave this place, Maim-ela. It's a wicked country.

—I won't leave, Tate, unless you come with us.

—You know we can't come. Momma is not well. And I'm an old man, it's not for us to start over in a new country. But you should go. You are young, you have your own life.

My mother-in-law stood in the doorway listening. —What are you telling them, Itzak? Their life is here, this is their country.

—No, Gussie. There's nothing anymore for Jews in this place.

—What nonsense, you have no faith. Times are good, times are bad, that's the way of the world. This too will pass. Do you think there will always be a war?

We was thinking the businesses would be taken and some other things will be taken by the Germans. They come to the house and help themselves to what they wanted, food, books, two quilts what my mother was making. The quilts were a wedding present my mother gave me, one was just a patch-work made from scraps of material, dark red, orange, brown, but the other was a scene from the village where I was grow-ing up. She made it with the road and the houses and on the top left corner was our house with the tree in front what was partly burned from the time in the storm. Always I kept that quilt on my bed and in the winter when it was very cold I was getting dressed underneath it. But the soldier yanked it from there, carried it from the house dragging on the ground. It was very long, he tripped and cursed and threw it onto the floor of the truck where another soldier stepped on it. My mother watched from the window, very anxious. —Where are they taking my quilts?

—It's the war, Momma. This is what happens.

MARISA KANTOR STARK

—No, the war is over, I remember a long time ago it ended. Go get my quilts, please, Maimela. I don't think I want him to have them.

—I can't get them for you now, Momma. Hush, it will be all right.

They took away my father's books, the chumash and even his siddur. The siddur was the hardest because it was keeping the history of our family. In the cover my father wrote all of our birthdays, me and my sister and my brother, and different things about our growing up. My brother's bar mitzvah parsha, the day I started cheder, my wedding date. All in neat careful letters with black ink. When Motti died he wrote that too but the letters was smaller and later when I open the book I see there's a tiny smudge there at the corner of the date. Now the book is gone, all that is lost. I can't remember no more what year my birthday was, 1901 or 1902, I don't know for sure. I'm terribly forgetful. It's lucky my name I still remember.

They took also our furs to send them to the Russian front.

We didn't like it, nobody liked it, but nobody thought what it would be. Only now, looking back, I think maybe my father knew. He didn't say nothing but I think he knew.

On Purim it was very cold. People was afraid to be going to the shul to hear the megillah so they were reading in the houses. We were gone to my husband's parents in the village and some people were there. They was reading downstairs.

Upstairs was two girls and they were hiding. They were from another village in a different part of Poland where the

Germans was stricter, it was a ghetto and later they maked there a labor camp.

One time at night they came to the ghetto and caught the people what was in the streets and they took them to the village by my in-laws. They brought them to the Jewish homes. To my in-laws there was two girls, cousins, about fourteen years old. They looked like twins.

Everyone was saying —What are they going to do with them, maybe kill them, maybe take them away at night. So my mother-in-law put them at night in the attic. It was very cold and she gave them quilts and blankets and said —Stay, this is where you will be safe. Downstairs we were crowding together around the table hearing the megillah, three, four families. —Read it loud, they said, —the girls should hear.

When they chased us from the house we went to stay by my in-laws in the village. Me, my husband, and my parents. The girls was gone.

                          MARISA KANTOR STARK

24

Once in this country on the street I saw a girl I think know from Poland and I ran to her. —Ethel, how did you get here, how did you survive? Tell me, and I grabbed her hand. So she was looking at me and she says in English —What are you saying? I don't understand. And I say —Weren't you in the war in Poland? and she says —No, I was born here.

But I can't believe, such a resemblance. It wasn't so long ago, I remember exactly how she looked. Pale skin, brown eyes. She walked like that even, with a limp leaning a little bit to the side. Her left leg was shorter. She lived just down the road to us and she used to come often to the house to borrow something from my mother, an egg or a cup of milk what her mother needed for baking. It was like no time was passed at all from the last time I saw her coming up the path. For a minute I forgot everything that happened, I was thinking we was the same people from what we were back then. But of course that's not true, we're very, very different now. If Ethel is still alive and I should see her probably I won't know her at all. I'm certain she will not know me.

Sometimes it's like that, for a little while you can forget. Like I wake up in the morning and my mind is empty from everything I've gone through and for a minute I am at peace. Or I'll be talking to some people and not thinking. But then all of a sudden it's there again on the edge of my mind, like the line of a shadow what you see from the side of your eye, and I know I'll never be without it. It is become a part of me. I'm lying in bed I feel it settle on my chest and I'm talking to people I break off to tell them —Do you know, I was living through the Second World War. Because I can't go without telling them. It is always there eating at the heart.

25

I have one friend what's still in Poland, but she don't know what is happened to me, that I'm here, because I can't write now no more. I had an address and Karyn says she will write, I should tell her what to say, but I can't find the address. I know my nephew took it. He don't want I should make a correspondence.

He said I should not be making calls. There's a phone in my room so he says —Tanta, you're making too many calls. But it's not true that I'm calling. Who is there I should call? I have a little phone book in my drawer with all the people what I knew but a lot of them the numbers are wrong now, they moved away someplace to live with children or a place like this, and I don't know where. Some names is crossed out with a marker, these are people what I heard somehow they passed away. And then there are some I can't remember who they are at all, I sit and look at the name and I try to think did I know this person once, and my mind is blank, I can't put a face there. That's the saddest of all, these people what disappear from my memory without even a sign. Sometimes I'll get a card in the mail or a letter and then I'll remember but other times nothing.

It's only Raisa I call. She sent me her phone number in Israel and now I can't write to her but sometimes I call. Last night I think it was when I called her.

—Raisa, I didn't hear from you for so long.

—Hello, who is this? I can't hear too good, who is this please?

—Raisa, darling, it's Maime. You remember me, your dear friend from before the war.

—Maime. Of course I know, don't be silly. You called me just a few days ago, remember?

I think she is confused, I didn't call to her in weeks. How can I call her, my nephew took away the phone and I just got it back. They told me it was broken, something with the wires, and for three days there was no phone in my room at all. I know it don't take that long to fix some wires. It was another one of his plans. When they brought it to me I told them —It's about time, I know your tricks, but they just looked at me and plugged it into the wall. They think I'm an old lady what don't know nothing but that's how they're wrong. I am smart, I figure things out.

There is a woman here what don't speak. She had a stroke so she can't move one side of her body and she can't talk at all. But she's a very bright woman, she understands everything. She's like me, coming from Europe. When she was young she

MARISA KANTOR STARK

was a doctor in Hungary for women what was pregnant or having a baby. So she knows what we went through in Europe. I can talk to her in Jewish like I talk to Raisa and she'll understand.

She talks to me with her fingers. Not everybody understands her but I understand and the nurses will come to me. —Maime, can you tell us please what Menka is saying. Like she was telling me about the sock, the green sock missing from her room. She says the one is in her drawer but the other one is gone without a clue. Well, I'm not surprised from this, the nurses must have took it. When they asked me I told them her sock is missing and they said probably it's lost in the wash. That's their excuse, they have to say something, but I'm sure they took it.

I was thinking if I could not speak what would I be. I should never know from it. I told my nephew —If ever I cannot speak I will want to die. He says —Tanta, don't talk like that, what things you're saying. There's never a day when you don't speak.

But I'm not joking, I am serious. Not to speak is like to be dead.

During the war when we were hiding we wasn't speaking but softly in a whisper. And if we were coughing or sneezing it was with our hands over our mouths to close it inside. My throat hurt from keeping back my voice and sometimes I thought I can't stand it no more, all this hushed voices. I wanted to scream and scream somebody should hear. Not words, it was just the sound I wanted to open outside myself and make a place for me in the world. It's me, Maime. Maimela they call me. I'm here, I'm still alive.

26

Once he told me Vicki will be to see me at ten o'clock. So I was sitting in this chair waiting for her and Karyn says —Come on inside the dayroom, Maime, there's a speaker about Israel. Well, I wanted very much to hear the speaker but I was sitting here, waiting for my nephew's daughter I shouldn't miss her. I would feel terrible if I will miss her and she's coming especially to see me. So I was waiting and through the glass I see the speaker, he was showing slides. They was places I remember seeing, I would love to look at those slides. It was eleven-thirty and still she don't come.

I go to my room to call. —Milton, where is she?

—Where is who, Tanta?

—What you mean who? Vicki, your daughter.

—Vicki's not coming today. Sunday I said she'll come.

—You said today.

—No, Tanta, she's not even home today, she went to New York. I said Sunday.

MARISA KANTOR STARK

He said today. You see how he twists the words. I'm an honest person, I can be saying something ten times it is the same. From my parents I learned to be honest with people. Because I remember one time when my brother was younger he was going with some Gentile children and he was learning from them to talk bad and be telling lies. My father, he knew this, and he told my brother not to go no more with those children. —In this family we tell only the truth. If you say something the truth, you aren't going to change it because it is the truth.

I always remember this what my father was saying. What you look at me is what I am and what you hear me is what I am.

On that Sunday morning she was coming, we sat outside on the benches. She wasn't changing none, she looks the same like she did when I stayed by my nephew. Vicki is dark like Milton with very straight hair down at her shoulders, not like mine what always had a little curl, and she's always patchking with it, smoothing a piece around her finger. She's a nice-looking girl, my husband's family is all that way.

—So, Tanta, how're you feeling? How's your head?

—I'm all right. Some days are bad, some days not so bad. Today is not so bad.

—That's good.

It was a warm day, other people was outside, and I saw her looking around at them. She's not used to what it is here, I think she was a little bit moved back when the lady in the wheelchair started making those noises like she does. It was once I was also frightened, staring at her tongue how it hangs out from her mouth like a dog, and I think to myself that can't be a woman's sound. But now I'm accustomed to it, it don't bother me no more. Hardly I notice it.

Vicki leaned over to take my hand. —It's good to see you, Tanta.

—Thank you. I appreciate you to come, I like to have visitors and see new people. Here it is always the same people. Not that I'm lonesome, you understand. Wherever I go I have people, I make friends.

—I know, of course. Well, this is a very nice place.

—Yes. So tell me something. Tell me how is your job? Your father says you have a very good job.

—Oh, I love it. I work for AT&T.

—What's this?

—AT&T? You know, the telephone company.

—Right, the telephone, that's what I thought. Do you make good money?

—Yeah, actually I do pretty well. I'm making around $30,000.

—That's very good. You're lucky to be born in this country. Are you married?

—You know I'm not married.

—I thought not. But you could be getting married. With that money you can start a family.

—God, I'm nowhere near ready to get married. I'm not even twenty-four.

—I was married I was seventeen. In Poland we were going boys and girls together. What are you twenty-three, twenty-four, you should be . . .

—Twenty-three.

MARISA KANTOR STARK

— . . . meeting Jewish boys. Maybe I know somebody. I'll ask Berta. She has a granddaughter something your age, it must be she knows Jewish boys you can meet.

—Tanta, please, I'm doing fine on my own. Listen, I have to get going. I think it's about time for your lunch.

—I'm not hungry. Come inside, I'll see if I can find Berta.

—You have to eat.

—Maybe you'll stay and eat with me? I can ask them to bring another tray.

—No thanks, not today. I'm meeting someone for lunch.

—You're sure? It would be very nice.

—No, really, I can't. I'm late already.

—Where you're going?

—I told you, I'm going out to lunch.

—Oh. That's very nice. Is it a kosher place where you're going?

—I don't know. Well, it was good to see you again, Tanta. Maybe I'll stop by some night on the way home from work.

She kissed my cheek. I stood up, holding my bag, and watched her go down the walk, get into a red car. She turned once to wave and I waved back. I kept waving while the car pulled out from the parking lot. Then it disappeared into the traffic on the streets and I couldn't see it no more but still I was standing there waving my hand. Waving and waving like I don't know how to stop.

27

After the war we came to America. We had some money left over from the American dollars I kept in Poland. Lia in New York wanted to give me twenty dollars but I won't take. I said —We have three hundred and fifty American dollars, and she says —There are people born in this country and they don't have that kind of money. So that's how it was.

With this money we was starting business. First we stayed some time by my nephew, he lived in Newark then, and I was watching his children. It was such hard work, at that time he had only two children but I never worked so hard in my life. All day I was alone with them in the apartment, Debbie had a job working in a school and my husband was working in a store for appliances. And I was a grown woman, past forty, past the age to be going after children. Later we got our own apartment not so far away. It was more a flat really, only one room with the brown corduroy couch in one corner that opened up to be a bed. We didn't have even a

MARISA KANTOR STARK

kitchen or an oven. I had two burners and with this I was cooking.

We had nothing, not a spoon or a fork. I was thinking they'll give us because the American consul was giving people what survived from the Hitlers tickets to come to America. But not for the house they wasn't giving nothing.

My nephew could have given us. He brought us tickets to America but these we could get ourselves from the consul, better he should have brought something for the apartment. Because before we came to this country I gave away everything. I didn't have much, you know, we was hiding, but what I had I gave to people, I didn't want to take nothing with us.

So I told them —In three days we're going to America and you can take this, this pillow, this blanket, this one pot. They were thinking now to take it and I said —No, not yet, we're living here three more days and after three days we're going to America. Then you can have everything, I don't need anything from this life in Poland.

When I come to America I was taking such things what other people throw away and use it for something. Like a glass from the candle, I maked some hot water to clean it and then it was a cup for tea. Or an old coffee can, I wiped it around and made it to keep sugar. The smell was always there, the sugar had a bitter taste like coffee, but we were using it and we were glad because we didn't have nothing.

So now I'm in this place here but if I see people what don't have nothing, not a fork even, I am helping them.

My husband had a sister what she was married in this country and she and her husband had a store in Newark. It was a yard goods store. They had this store twenty-five years and they can't make it good, my brother-in-law wanted to sell. I saw he had a sign there in the window and I asked him about it. —For two years now I have this sign and nobody wants to buy. Uch, it's a bad business.

Me and my husband were going to look. I was standing in the store, I don't know good English, but I saw a lady what she wanted to buy fabric for a dress. She picked a fabric, red with little green squares, and my brother-in-law says —Are you sure this is the one you want, can't you find a better fabric? Because he didn't know to run a store. They were American people, my sister-in-law married an American man, and they don't know the first thing to run a business.

Well, I picked out a fabric, a dark green with a wave pattern, and I was going over to the lady. —This is a nice fabric. You like this one?

I put it against her. —It goes nice with your hair.

—You think so?

She took it to the mirror, twisted to see herself from different sides. —You know, I think you're right, it's a good color for me. I'll take it.

Then she looked at my dress what I'm wearing and it was a very nice dress. —Where can I get it made into a dress like that?

I told her —This dress I sewed myself, if you like I can sew for you a dress.

I took the fabric and made the dress and she was paying me good, she was very pleased.

My husband says —Jack, what if we'll buy this store.

—Well, I don't know. I hate to . . . It's not much of a business.

—We'll make it a business.

—I don't know, Saul. I tried that.

—You have someone else?

—Nah, I told you, I can't find anyone else.

—So then. I'll give you fifty dollars now and the rest you'll get after we make money.

—It doesn't seem right somehow. A stranger now that would be different but you're family.

—Jack, I'm telling you it's all right. I take responsibility.

—Well then. But I'm real sorry, it's not much of a business.

Did we make a store. They didn't make half what we were making. First it was only the yard goods but then I thought to myself why not dresses so after a few years we started to have dresses. Maime's Dress Shop on Clinton Avenue and people come there from all over, even from the bigger stores they was coming to us. We had one customer what worked at a department store but she came to us to buy her dresses. They weren't so expensive dresses, just the kind you can wear around for different things. It maked a very fine business.

My husband was a good businessman. He had excellent taste, he knew to buy what people were wearing. I was thinking myself to go but it was hard, there was so many kinds of styles I don't know what to buy. One time I go, I come back, I tell my husband   I can't decide. Should I get the very long or the not-so-long? I think the very long is too long.

—So what did you get?

—Nothing. I can't decide.

But my husband always knew. He was going around to the wholesale stores, you know, if you want to be successful in business you can't go to only one store. He came back with the dresses, I was looking what he got. —You got the long. Don't you think they're too long? Nobody will buy so long.

—That's the style. They're wearing them long.

—Not this long, Saul. You'll see, nobody will buy that dress.

But they was buying. They came in and it was the first one they buy, everybody wanted that dress. Such a style, they say, so long and slim.

Because it don't matter what I like, a Jewish person, it's what the Gentiles like and what they're buying.

The customers liked my husband. If a woman will try a dress, she calls him —Come here, help me button this dress. So he was thinking not to go, it was a closet, a fitting room, where the women were trying it. But then if he wasn't coming she says —What, do I have something you haven't seen before? I want you to help me here. And he had to go.

I taught my husband to sew and we started to make alterations. Fixing a hem, a sleeve, we hanged the dress on the hooks in the back while we did the sewing. The store was open until nine o'clock but on Thursdays we were closing early at six and that was the day we stayed to do the alterations. Until eleven o'clock sometimes we stayed. I had in the back there a little kitchen and I did the baking what I couldn't do in the apartment. So then the store smelled like baking and the dresses smelled like my mother's dresses when she took them off and hanged them to air in her bedroom and I'd come in and press my face to the cloth. People came to the store. —Mmm . . . what smells so good? Because the Gentiles were never smelling such a good bread. It was Jewish bread.

We had another woman working for us, a salesgirl what worked in the store for my brother-in-law. She was a very nice girl to sit and talk to her and such but she had no business sense. She was showing them the new dresses what just came in and I said —What you're showing these dresses, first show

MARISA KANTOR STARK

the ones what are hanging there. After we sold the store she was gone to work someplace else but I heard from some people she wasn't there too long.

In my business I was very honest. A woman was coming in so I tell her —This looks good for you, this is not so good. One woman says —I want a dress like your dress, and she's a size 40. And I say —This dress is an eight/ten and you're a 38 so it can't be we're having the same dress, how about this other one. That's how it was and they were trusting to me. Because why should I tell her it looks good if it don't look good, and then somebody else will be telling her. So they came back to the store and brought us more customers.

I let them buy with a credit. If a woman bought a dress and she can't pay for it, let's say thirty dollars, just for example. So I call up and they were telling me —This woman you can trust for such and such amount of money. Then I let her pay it off a little bit each time, five dollars this week, five dollars the next week. But in the meantime she's buying another dress. That's how our business grew.

We had so many customers, I don't have the time what to spend with them. There was one woman she used to come in, try all the different dresses and still not buy nothing. I go to help another customer and she says —I'm here first, this other lady came not half an hour ago. —Yes, I say, —she came, she bought four dresses, and now she's leaving, and you, you are still here. Then she said —Well, now I'm ready to buy, which one should I take? And she would hold them up, take them back to the fitting room to try them all again.

There's all kinds of stories working in a store. I remember another woman, not a regular customer, what she came to the store with a wedding dress with two left sleeves. In those days people were not having this many fancy dresses like today, they had one and they wore it to all the different occasions. So this woman had one nice dress what she was wearing for her wedding. But it had no sleeves and the wedding was in a church and the priest, he was a very religious man, said it needs sleeves. Her aunt sewed for her some sleeves. Only she made them two left sleeves, and of course she can't be wearing it like that, she brought it to me I should fix it. Well, I can't imagine what she thought I can do with two left sleeves. So I had to make all new sleeves. Then the old ones I was thinking to throw away but she wanted to keep them for a souvenir, I shouldn't tear them or nothing. She folded them and took them with her. To remember by, she said.

❀   ❀   ❀

We had a cat in the store. She was appearing suddenly one morning at the stoop and I can't get rid of her, black with white like a mask around the face and the top of one of her ears missing. I gave her milk in a little dish outside the door.

—Maime, what are you doing, if you feed her she won't ever leave. I don't want a cat here.

—Well, I also don't want but what can I do?

—Don't feed her.

—She can't be going hungry. She has no place to go.

—I'm telling you she'll never leave.

In Poland we always had a cat for the mice, we called her Tupchkin or Tupchka. So this cat I also named Tupchka.

She stayed by the store drinking the milk and sleeping. If I come outside she was turning on her back, you know, with her legs in the air I should scratch her stomach. When it was getting cold then sometimes I let her inside the store in the back by the oven. I spread a blanket for her there on the floor.

—Maime, inside here? She'll ruin the dresses.

But one time I saw him bend over and scratch her stomach. He thought I'm not watching but I saw.

If people was coming to the store I was asking them —Do you want a cat? but nobody wants. And she stayed.

Somebody came here with a cat. It was gray and bigger than Tupchka and the nurse asked me —Maime, do you want to hold her? She put her on my lap and I touched her carefully with the tip of my finger. I thought I was forgetting what it will feel like but some things you just don't forget. What it feels to touch a cat.

28

It wasn't easy to have that store, work all the time and come home late. But I didn't mind it, I needed to be all the time busy, filling the days so there was no time for nothing else. I was glad to feel only the hurt in my body, fall to sleep too tired to think. With this work I was building again my life.

All what I had I threw to making this new life. I had a girl what came to the apartment to teach me English. She was eleven years old and her mother was a Russian woman I was dealing business with her. We got to be friendly and she said —My daughter goes to school, she can help you to learn English. So at night after I got back from the store I maked dinner for me and my husband and then at ten o'clock she was come to teach me a lesson.

She had different books she brought. They were story books, romances she called them, not about real people or real life. Well, that's fine for a young girl but I'm a grown person, I survived through the war, what do I need these stories. So after a time I say to her —I want to read something real, I want to read the newspaper. I told my husband —We need to buy a newspaper, and then when she was coming she helped me to read it. I read everything, the news, the business, all the advertisements. If I don't have time to finish a newspaper I was saving it until Shabbos when we didn't do no work and the store was closed and then I take out all the papers from the week and go through it. The girl is saying there's no purpose to save them, it's old news, but I don't care I just want to read and to learn.

It was in these newspapers I found about President Eisenhower. All this time I'm thinking his name is White Eisenhower and I thought this is strange he should have a name what's also a color, who can say how they're doing in this country. But then she showed me in the paper it's not White it is Dwight. President Dwight Eisenhower. If you say it all together it sounds like White.

I gave the girl a quarter she should buy herself something. Her mother said —No, you don't have to, but I don't take nothing from nobody, I want to give her. I know they don't have so much money, she can use it. A candy maybe or a ribbon for her hair.

After she left I'd sit by the table, sounding the words and copying them with a pencil I should learn to write. I had a little light burning in the kitchen. I was very tired, the letters on the page were become dark spots moving back and forth in front of my eyes. But I drink coffee, push myself to go on.

My husband was already asleep. He don't want the lessons, he said —I'm dealing in business, I'll learn there what I need to learn. Because he wasn't used to studying, in Poland he went only a short time to school. He learned a little bit to read

English from the store but if it was something not too simple he'd ask me —Maime, I want to be sure what this says. He read the Jewish paper. And to each other we was talking always in Jewish.

So still today I don't know good English. But I look around me, what does it matter. There are people what were born in this country all their life and they're also here with me in this place.

MARISA KANTOR STARK

29

We had a very good accountant, me and my husband. He was
a religious man and a smart man, he came by us to eat because
he knew I was kosher. And he used to say —Don't be saving
a hundred dollars, the more you pay the more your social
security will be in old age. Because the years was passing,
we had to start thinking about the future. But my husband
don't want none to listen to him. He's always thinking he
knows better.

—Why I should give my money to the government?

—I'm telling you in the long run it will be worth it. You'll
thank yourself for it. You'll thank me.

—Saul, listen to him, he knows what he's saying. He's a
smart man.

—I rather we keep the money.

—No. Always you with the money. I'm telling you now, this
money I won't let you keep.

—What do you mean, this money? What other money are we talking about here?

—You understand what I'm saying. The money I wanted to send to the Polish man.

—What's that to do with anything, Maime? We sent him money. It was you insisted we send it, if I remember.

—Not enough. I would have sent him more. We didn't give him even one percent what he deserved.

—My Gott, Maime, what do you want? We also need to live. I told you a hundred times he was a shikkur, he only spent what you sent him at the taverns.

—And now he's dead, we can't send him anymore.

—That's right, he's dead. It's over, finished.

—No, Saul, it's not ever finished. You know that same as I do.

After six years working in the store we had enough money we could retire. But still I kept working and making money. I had an account at Bamberger's. My husband says —What do you need that for, you always make your own clothes, but I wanted such an account. It makes me feel how I am something again, I have things. We got another apartment in a different neighborhood, a nice, big apartment one flight up with a view to the park. It was a lovely park. I remember when we first moved there I asked a woman —What are those beautiful yellow flowers growing in the grass? and she laughed and told me they're not flowers, those are weeds. Dandelions is how she called them, and people don't grow them, they try to be rid of them. But to me they're very pretty, like little yellow

MARISA KANTOR STARK

suns in the grass. I wouldn't mind to have some in a pot for my window.

When first we came to the apartment, I was walking through the rooms. They were all white with nothing inside, the furnitures wasn't come yet, and my feet was making a loud lonely sound on the wood floors. The whole air smelled like new paint.

—It's brand new, they just painted it, my husband told me.

I look around. —They dripped some paint. Look, on the floor there.

—That doesn't matter. We'll get a nice rug for it.

—But it feels so empty, Saul. I don't know that I like it.

—You will like it. With the rug and the new furniture, it will be different.

But when the things come still there is something wrong with the apartment. A few days I'm walking around there, try to feel what is it, why am I disturbed. Then I see it's the paint.

—The paint? My husband stares at me. —What's wrong with the paint?

—It's too white. It looks like a hospital.

—That's ridiculous. I don't know where you find these ideas.

—I'm going to paint it again.

—It's a waste, Maime. All this new paint.

—I don't care. I won't live in a place that looks like a hospital.

I got a stepladder and two days I painted the whole apartment. Cream, it's softer from white, and also a rose. I was wearing one of Saul's old shirts, it was down to my knees like a dress. I don't mind the work. I like the smooth way it feels to move the brush across the walls. I was very careful, I spread a sheet on the floor to hold the drips. But there is paint in my hair, that I can't help it, and for a long time afterwards even I was washing my hair I'm finding a piece of it.

Once he comes in, stands shaking his head. —All this work and money. A complete waste. I make like I don't hear him and he goes away. While I paint I'm humming a little bit of music. I don't know where it came from like that, a melody without no words. Something I remember from back in Poland.

❋   ❋   ❋

In that neighborhood where we were moving was a settlement of black Jews. I never knew there's such a thing like a black Jew. There was one man, I know he was Jewish because I saw him walking with a yarmulke and such, but I didn't know he was black. He was a doctor and he don't look black but then I saw black people was going to him so I knew. People were telling me —Yes, there's a whole apartment house of them. Isn't that something. Whenever I see him I say hello and he picks up his hat and says hello back to me and this way we are friendly. I talk to all kinds of people.

I always had people coming to the apartment. The building had dryers, in a room in the basement, and I would meet people there. I wasn't used to drying the clothes this way, I prefer better to hang them outside, and the first time I'm putting all the clothes together at one time in the dryer. A woman with her hair made up with bobby pins was pulling things from a different dryer. She turned to me.

—I don't mean to stick my nose in, but they'll never dry that way. Better to put them in two machines.

—Oh, thank you, this I didn't know. All my life I'm hanging my laundry.

MARISA KANTOR STARK

—I know. I used to do that too, hang out the sheets. They smelled so good.

—Yes, yes, you remember? Like wind and leftover sun. I love to sleep on them, they make such nice dreams.

—Did you just move in? My name's Lou. Apartment 3C. I don't usually go out with my hair like this, but if you leave your things in the dryer after it stops somebody takes them out and just dumps them on the floor. You should keep that in mind when you do laundry, make sure you're here when your clothes are done.

—Thank you. I will remember.

I invite her up to my apartment. And also other women I was talking and having them up. —Such a nice place you have here, Maime, you fixed it up so pretty.

They was amazed at my violets. —And what flowers! I've never seen them like this before. How do you do it, how do you grow them so nice?

—There's a way. The right water, the right light. I learn from experience.

—I wish I could have plants like that. I had a violet once, I think it was a violet, but I dropped it from the fire escape. After that it never had another flower no matter what I did.

I told her violets are like people. You can't shock them like that then expect they'll go on like nothing is happened. Something inside them is changed and can't be changed back. I was always very careful to my plants.

I sold the store to two Italian girls what was to us very good customers. It was enough, I didn't want it no more, I was letting myself to go slower some and not work this hard. I was almost sixty, and my husband was already sixty-four, sixty-five. His hand was shaking a little bit, it wasn't easy for him to hold the needle. So when the girls heard I was selling they're talking together they will buy. Because whenever they was come to the store it's filled with customers and they thought this is some business. But these girls, they don't know nothing to run a store, they were fighting like cats. People were telling me —Maime, it's changed, it's just not what it was, and after two months they closed it up.

Because the neighborhood now is not what it used to be. Even when I was living there it was changing some, the Jewish people moving out, other people moving in what don't live the way we do. Lou, she lives there still, was whispering to me —Maime, it's practically all black, telling me how she won't never go out at night and her children wants her to move. And my nephew, always talking to me that it's dangerous. There are people robbed on the streets, he said, and children taking knives in the schools.

Well, it's not so dangerous like that. They exaggerate everything. But it's true things are not the same. It's not my place no more.

MARISA KANTOR STARK

30

I'm not rich but I have. I think the pension what I get from the Germans is more than the social security. It's a check for seven hundred dollars for me and my husband. But my nephew takes the money, he's using it to pay. I don't know if it's enough, maybe yes maybe no, let's say yes. Then I'd like very much to know what about the rest.

One time he was coming here with the books and in the books I see he's not writing the pension. Only the social security. So I don't know if he tells them even about the pension. The social security, you understand, this is American and he cannot hide it but my pension I know he's keeping it for himself.

Well, I don't tell them nothing because they'll put him in trouble, maybe in jail. It's all right they should be getting only the social security. They think this is all I have and if a person don't have so they're not putting them out to the street.

But he takes my money and I'm not getting from him nothing. I have to ask him one day I need a bra, the clasps on my other one is broken, and I'm not used to this, to discuss about women's clothing with a man. In my store I had some bras because if you don't have the right thing underneath the dress isn't looking good. So sometimes a woman will try a dress and I see it's sagging so I tell her —Here, try it with this other bra. You'll see what it makes a difference. But it was only to the women I was talking this. And now there's not left to me no other choice, I have to tell him. He don't buy for me a pair of stockings. Every night I'm washing my stockings and put them out on the chair to dry. But in the morning it was gone so now I put them under the pillow. First I wrap them in the towel they shouldn't get wet and then I tuck them inside the pillowcase. Because people take things. The nurses here are anti-Semites.

He gave away my clothes. Isn't it something, they all wear my same size, all his daughters. So I have only this one clothes, at night I wash it and in the morning I wear it. People are noticing. Karyn, she says —Maime, every day you wear that same old thing. She don't know I used to have beautiful clothes. But I go out, my nephew comes to the room and he takes whatever he's looking in the closet. I don't hide nothing because I'm not the type. I am not an American person, I'm a very honest person. He says he's taking them to be cleaned.

I'm not going to ask for nothing. I don't expect nothing, I don't ask. It's just not the same nephew what it was. If this skin on my arm was money what he can take, he'd take it.

Once he was here I heard him talking. It was to Karyn and I can't understand all what they're saying but something I hear. — . . . oh, I'm glad . . . it's good for her to . . . you know sometimes it's hard . . .

MARISA KANTOR STARK

I know he was talking about me. That it's hard to be keeping me here and such because I'm an old woman past ninety and it's a lot of money. He likes it better I should be dead.

What can I do. I told this to Berta, she said talk to him. But there's not too much to talk. He can say something, my nephew, what will go through and through me. He has two son-in-laws lawyers, one in England and one in this country. He can make all kinds of papers. I need to have a lawyer like that. And he has an excuse. He's paying here I don't know how much.

❧ ❧ ❧

—Tanta, Karyn tells me how you help out a lot around here. I'm really glad, it's good for you to be keeping busy.

—I'm not so busy.

—Oh, you must be. She said you help with feeding people, setting up the dining room. I hear you're even doing some baking for the bake sale. You've sure got lots of mitzvahs.

—No, I don't think so, Milton. I don't know how many mitzvahs I have.

—Sure you do. How many mitzvahs did you do today? I'll bet you did plenty for people just today.

—I'm telling you, I don't have no mitzvahs. If I had mitzvahs I wouldn't be in this place.

—No, Tanta? Where would you be?

He said it just like that, looking at me with his dark eyes very straight and serious. I have no answer. And suddenly I know how it is.

I am trapped.

I felt a fear come to my chest like a wave, taking my breath. This is it, I thought, the end. This is how everything comes to, sitting in a black vinyl chair outside the dayroom, the fish moving back and forth behind the glass. I start to wonder, do those fish know they have walls, can they see outside I'm sitting here, or maybe they think the whole world is rocks and plants and a little plastic diver floating in the water. I don't know which way is better, to know or not know.

I pray soon Gott will see good to take me. When you're young you pray to live but now, now it is the opposite.

31

But I worry when I die who will say Kaddish. Right now I say
for my husband and for my parents. I go to the shul here to
say it. It's not a shul really, they have a room by the dining
room what they call a sanctuary. I don't like it. They set up
chairs and the people come, sit wherever, not like a real shul
where the men and women are separate and there's a curtain.
The room is small with wood panels and only one window up
very high with pieces of colored glass like a church.

At one end is the aron with the Torah, this Torah is the only
real thing about the shul. Because it comes from Europe,
Czechoslovakia, it survived from the war and somebody was
bringing it here to this country. The cover is sewed from hand
from different pieces of material, all shapes and colors. There's
a green chicken made of felt and gold satin coins and a bush
burning with purple and orange flames. They say it was a
whole group of women from one community came together
in the houses to sew it, each one with her own design.

It must be those women are all dead now. But I think I can know how they were like, sitting together around the table with the material spread out in front of them. They are different ages, maybe some mothers with their daughters, and every one is different, the stitches are different. Some are very small neat stitches you can hardly see them and then some are big and a little bit messy like from a young girl what she's not so experienced. While they work they talk about their lives. So I know a little part of them is left in the cloth and this gives to me a special feeling, like they left it for me to find. Sometimes when nobody is around I come to the sanctuary to the aron and I open it to look at the Torah, touch the cover ever so lightly. Then afterwards I kiss my fingers.

Over the aron is hanging a ner tamid with a reddish light and in front is the table where the rabbi stands when he comes. This rabbi has a face like a moon, very round and pale with marks in it, and he's always having a joke. Every week he gets to the part of the davening before the amidah, he says —Now we'll do an old Chinese folk song, mi chamocha. He laughs loud, his stomach shaking, and some other people laugh. I don't know are they laughing just to laugh or do they think he's funny. I don't never laugh. He shouldn't make jokes like that about the davening. This is a Hebrew prayer, me kamoka, and it's about the greatness of Gott.

I'm a religious person, not so religious no more now like I used to be, but still I come from a very religious home. I wish for Gott to forgive me, it's not so easy here to be religious. Shabbos isn't Shabbos like I maked it in my own home.

The Shabbos davening they have here Friday morning. Because Friday night it's too late, the people go to sleep at six-thirty, and Saturday there's too much visitors. So I see the rabbi, I know it must be Friday, I can't believe it already, to me it seems we just had a Friday. It's ridiculous to daven like this in the morning I tell him. Shabbos don't start until dark. But he just smiles at me and wipes his forehead with a handkerchief. He has two three handkerchiefs in all his pockets and he's always pulling them, wiping his head and his neck. He's a big man, he gets very hot.

And the davening is not how it should be, it's a lot in the English. The rabbi says the Kiddush and passes some grape juice in plastic cups together with a little piece of challah. Not real challah, it's white and crumbly and tastes like dust. I remember once when Berta was making ready to eat it her teeth fell out to the floor, right there in the shul. She can't bend to get them and a nurse had to crawl between the chairs. Some people didn't see but I was sitting behind her so I saw. For a minute she turned around and I saw her mouth without the teeth, a black hole with the lips falling in. It was a terrible thing and without thinking I put my hand to my own mouth but then quickly I move it down she shouldn't notice me. And later I don't say nothing to her about it. Berta's my friend, I won't want to make her feel bad.

Holidays also are not the same. At home it was weeks we spent preparing for the chag, getting ready the baskets of food to bring them to the poorer people. We put bread, cakes, may be some jam. On Pesach especially we was busy cleaning and changing over everything. Even the clothes we changed and my mother maked us new dresses for spring. But here on Pesach I didn't know till the morning and then when I went to my closet I had nothing to wear. I had to wear again this flowered dress. I noticed it has a button missing on the bottom, somebody must have cut it off. I can tell from the way the threads are hanging.

But to all this I don't never miss a time the rabbi comes. I have to say Kaddish. It used to be I knew all the siddur by heart but now I wait for what he is saying. He says the words then he stops we should say after him. Because almost everybody has someone for what they say.

A lot of people don't know you are supposed to stand. Some of them is in a wheelchair but there are some can stand if they want to, if somebody was telling them. So I tell them. I make with my hand they should get up and then some of them do but others are sitting with a blank face like they don't understand nothing what I'm saying. Well, after that there's no more I can do, if they won't stand they won't stand, it's not my business to be forcing them. I always stand. If I need two people to hold me still I'll stand for the Kaddish.

I wonder will my nephew say Kaddish for me. Really it's supposed to be a closer relative, a wife for a husband, a child for a parent, or the other way. He's not my relative even, he's my husband's nephew, and I know I can't trust him. He's not much a religious person, he don't go to shul except on the big holidays like Yom Kippur and he don't know to read Hebrew. He has a painting in his house with Hebrew letters and one time when I was there he asked me to read it to him. So I can see how it will be, how he'll get busy and forget to say.

But there's no one else. I don't have no other family.

32

It used to be I had some family, I had my sister in this country. But she passed away after my husband passed away. I was sick then, it was after my operations while I was staying by my nephew, and I didn't go to her funeral. She has three children in New York but I don't see them, I don't call. They don't call me.

When I came to this country Lia wanted I should come live with her instead of with my nephew. She says —Maime, he's not even from your family, I'm your sister for Gott's sake. But I know what she was thinking. She thought I will do for her, clean, cook, so she can help her husband in his business. He was dealing with junk, people was bringing him metals and he melts them and sends them to factories. It was a good business, everyone has junk. He said to my husband —You can work for me, but my husband is looking to start his own business, he don't want to be working for another man. And also me, I don't want to keep my sister's apartment. This is like living with in-laws and in Poland in my own house I always had a maid.

I remember how she said she will send for me and she don't never send. If I came to this country before the war, things would be different. I'd have another husband, another life. An apartment maybe in the city where my children will grow up with other Jewish people. In the summers I'd send them to a Jewish camp, in the mountains I think, where the boys and girls are going together, meeting this one and that one. And my parents, they'd come with me and I'd have for them a place nearby. Or if first they don't come then for sure when the war started I would send for them. Before it's too late I'd go myself to bring them.

Lia could have done like that. I don't know why it was different, why she let it happen this way. I can't never take it from my mind. She sat here in her apartment in America and we didn't hear from her nothing. Well, almost nothing. At the start of the war there was a letter. —If you need anything I can send to you, just let me know. And then much later she wrote to me —The war is dragging on too long, the best thing is for you to get out of Poland. But that letter was lost, she sent it to the house in town and we was already left to go back with my in-laws. By the time I received it, the Germans was a few days from the village.

—We didn't know what was happening, she tells me. —We had no idea.

We were sitting together in the kitchen of her apartment, the sun slanting a line between us like a knife. She talks to me in English.

—I had to bring them, Lia. Bring us die alt war, zum Schiessen, they said. Bring us the old people so we can kill them.

—My Gott. My little sister. I don't know how you can live with yourself now.

MARISA KANTOR STARK

—What choice is there? I have no choice except to live.

—Did you think . . . maybe you could hide them.

—No.

—It seems there would be some way. I don't know. Well, don't look to me like that, Maime. I'm not saying nothing.

I get up, move to the window. It is steamy. I clear a little place and stand looking down to the street, at the people passing with bags and dogs and children. They are bent into their coats and their hands in their pockets and they look to me small and gray and far away. I'm surprised to see them there busy with their lives. Inside the kitchen it is like everything is stopped, like me and Lia is the only people in the world.

Before I saw her I was thinking it will be some kind of relief to talk to Lia. Because even through my anger I know she must carry it like I carry it, what we did, what we had to do. She's the only one, she who stood Friday night under my father's right hand while I stood under the left. Because they was her parents, too. That at least there was between us.

But when I talked to her this afternoon I saw I was wrong. She went over to the stove, stirs something in a pot. —Can you believe, the newspapers didn't say a word. There was some little things, but nothing really, nothing different from any kind of war.

I stare at her back. The way her shoulders curve, my mother's shoulders was like that.

She touches the wood spoon to her lips. —Not that I could do much if I knew. I mean what can I have done.

I realized we aren't closer for this, it's the opposite, we're farther away than ever.

For her it is something outside herself and for me, for me it's become the center of my heart. And I see it can't be no other way. To the end it was me what brought them to the square. No one else can know from it, not even I tell them, not even a sister. It was me what left them, my mother calling to my back, and went away to live through my life.

33

I will tell you something horrible. I can't remember my parents' faces. I mean little pieces I remember, my mother's hair, the small cracks in my father's hands. But I can't put them together to make what to hold on to. I try to remind myself, I lie in bed and try to build the picture again behind my eyes, but it slips away, falls apart before I can see it. The pieces sliding off in the dark. I don't have even a photograph to look at.

One time I was here in the library looking for a book. I like books about real people and I was looking for such a one, not too long, and inside the pages I found a photograph. It was Lou and Herman a long time ago, before Herman came here to this place, before he was like he is now. It must be Lou was coming to visit him and she took a book and inside she left a picture, maybe to mark the place.

I took the photograph and put it in my bag with my things, I should give it to her when I see her. Sometimes I take it out to look at it. They was such a couple, always fashionable and well-dressed. They used to travel a lot. In the picture they're wearing white shorts and Herman has sunglasses and a big hat. There are some very nice palm trees. They are tan.

Then I can't find it. I was looking and looking but I can't find it and I was telling Lou when she comes —I have a picture of you but somebody took it, it's gone. But then some weeks later my bag was torn, I caught it on the hook in the closet and it ripped, and when I was taking the things out I found the picture. I gave it to Lou and she kissed it. Because she has other pictures but not this one and she wanted to keep it to remember how things used to be.

What I would give to have such a picture like what I was finding. Of the house I have but that's all.

To look at him now you'll never guess Herman was once the same like me. He had a store where he was selling valises and they lived very good. We were very friendly together, him and Lou with me and my husband. They were coming downstairs to the apartment and we played cards. It was Herman's favorite game, he taught us to play bridge. So Saturday nights after Shabbos we would get together to play and I would bake a cake, make some coffee, maybe put out a piece of fruit or a bit of cheese. Or if Lou made chocolate cookies then she was bringing them on a plate. She was a good baker, not like me, but good. We played and then finally it was late and they went upstairs to bed.

MARISA KANTOR STARK

So you see I always had many friends.

Of course there was some times it wasn't so smooth, my husband and Herman don't always get along. Because Saul took the game very seriously and Herman didn't understand that, how he was getting angry if I don't do the bid right or I play the wrong card. —There's no reason to get so riled up, he said and then my husband told him —This is something what don't concern you, Herman, I'll thank you to keep out from it. So Herman said —No, it does concern me, if this is how you're playing I had enough for tonight, and he was taking his cards and going from the table. For a few weeks we stopped playing but then I invite them again and Lou convinces him he should come. And he liked cards and he liked me so he came.

He always wore a hat. He says it's to hide he's going bald and he had all different kinds hanging on hooks in the hall to the apartment. Brown felt hats, straw hats for summer, a top hat even, for a nice occasion.

Now he's all bald. He wears that dirty gray flannel shirt with missing buttons and he forgets to swallow so his mouth drools. Sometimes there's a little drip shining from the end of his nose. And he has something attached on his clothes what makes a noise if he passes by the door, he shouldn't some day just walk outside and they won't know. A lot of people here have such a beeper like that. I was always lucky, I never had one. For me it was always easy to go out.

First when Herman got sick he was in the hospital. But that was only for a short time and then he came here, so I was coming with Lou from the apartment to visit him. We brought cards, he should play something.

—How are you feeling today, Herman? Look, I brought you a deck of cards. Let's play solitaire.

She spread them on his tray. —See, here's the ten of hearts. What can you put on the ten?

—I'm hungry.

—How about a nine? See if you can find a nine.

He was taking a card.

—No, it has to be a nine. That's a six. Find a black nine.

—I don't want to. There is no nine. When we're going to eat?

When Milton brought me here the first room they gave me was two doors from Herman. But right away I saw I can't stay there. He used to come all the time looking for Lou and at night I heard him banging on the walls. I told Karyn —I can't sleep, will you listen to that noise, and after a few times I complained, they gave me a different room.

That was fine for some small time but now I know he found also this new room, because my red toothbrush is missing from the cup on the sink and he's the only one would have taken it. Even the nurses don't want an old toothbrush. It's a good thing I have an extra, I always keep an extra toothbrush if one will be stolen or fall to the floor. I asked them can I have a lock for the door, he shouldn't come and take something else, but they said —Nobody took nothing from you, Maime, you just misplaced it. They don't want for me to lock the door, then they can't come in whenever.

Lou comes all the time to visit Herman and she always stops to talk to me. —How are you, Maime, look what I brought you. Last week she had cookies in a blue tin container with snowflakes on it. She don't make the cookies like she used to, they're too sweet and I can't eat them. But I don't want to hurt

MARISA KANTOR STARK

her feelings, you know. So I put them in my drawer behind the stockings and the underwear. I keep them there nobody should find them. I was thinking I can give them to my nephew, he likes sweet things, but why should he have my cookies. It was for me what she made them. I always liked her, we're always good friends.

34

My husband had Parkinson's. For ten years he was terribly sick
and I was taking care of him in the apartment. First it was just
his hands shaking, I see it when he's lifting a cup or doing
something. He don't want we should talk about it and I pretend not to see but it keeps getting worse. I saw how long it
takes him to put on his shoes or close a zipper and finally I
can't keep quiet no more. —Saul, you should see a doctor.

—I told you it's nothing. I don't need a doctor.

—I don't know. Maybe he'll give you some medicine.

—What medicine? I'm getting older, Maime, we're both
getting older. I don't need to pay money for a doctor to tell
me this.

He walked now bent over at the waist and always he was a
tall man, very good-looking. Such dark hair he had. Do you
know, till the day he died he had all his hair.

Then one night he fell. We was sitting at the table in the
kitchen and the telephone rang, my husband was getting up

to answer it. But his foot slipped. I saw him reach out for the chair, the chair sliding away, and before I can move he is falling. —Saul!

He was on the floor, crumpled like a heap of clothes with no man inside. I bent over him.

—I'm all right. My arm a little . . . get the telephone.

—Forget the phone. What about your arm? Can you bend it? I helped him sit on the chair.

—I'm fine, fine. The stupid phone. Why didn't you answer it, now I missed the call.

—So they'll call back. They know where to find us.

—That's not the point they should call back. You should have answered it. I said to answer it.

He sat looking angry to the wall.

But in the morning while I was getting dressed he came in to me. He says like he has some new idea —Maime, I think maybe I'll see a doctor. Who knows, it could be there's some kind of medicine.

—Yes, that could be. Ask Milton about it, he'll know a good doctor.

I didn't say nothing because some things I learn it's easier to keep quiet, this way there is more peace in the home, and there are times it's not worth to argue. You're going to stay with a man you have to know this.

They gave him, what was it, Sinemet. It made him look funny, his lips twisting and his eyebrows moving up and down. He couldn't control it and he used to get terribly angry. Once I invited some people and he was shouting at me —How can you have people when I look like a clown? He stayed in the bedroom and didn't come out, I had to say he was sick. Then another time I'm feeding him and the food dropped from his mouth, he threw the bowl across the kitchen. It broke against the sink. I swept it up but I missed some pieces and the next day a piece went in my foot. I couldn't find it to get it out but if I'm walking I feel it. So I'm waiting for it to come out by itself.

I won't let myself to be depressed. I tell him —Give it time, it will get better, and always I was talking like everything is all right. Because that's the only way to manage it, tell yourself things someday will change. If you can believe that so then you can go on. It's when you stop thinking that way, when you know this is what it will be for the rest of my life, you start to ask the questions. What's it for, what reason there is to keep on living.

The medicine didn't work. For a short time things will be better, then they get worse again. He sits in a chair, his whole body shakes. At night he lies in the bed and his arms and legs move around in the bed like a puppet with someone pulling the strings. Only when he finally falls to sleep is he resting still.

My nephew was saying maybe it's too much for me. —You're not a hundred percent yourself, Tanta, with the headaches you're having lately. Let me find someplace for him.

—No.

—Look, I know a nice place, it's kosher. It's very close by, you can go over every day if you want to see him.

—What it's called?

—I don't remember, a friend of Debbie's was telling us about it. She said it has excellent facilities.

—Edgewood, maybe?

—Yeah, I think that's it. Edgewood Manor. You know it?

—Herman, the man from upstairs, is there. I go sometimes with his wife to visit.

—See, it's a nice place, right? I say we look into it.

—Milton, I'm not putting my husband to a place called Edgewood.

—What's wrong with the name? That's not a reason.

—No, Milton. It's not for him. He's my husband, I'll take care of him here.

❊ ❊ ❊

In all the years Saul won't never say I am right. This was the way he was brought up, not to be too much affectionate. In my own family it was entirely different, my parents always showed to each other love. My father will come up behind my mother, touch her cheek, tell her how beautiful she looked. And to me also, he said I'm growing up to be like her. But with my in-laws it wasn't this way. Well, every family does how it does. I got used to it.

But when he was sick so suddenly he starts to tell me things.

The first time was about the perfume. I remember very clearly I was going out to a Hadassah meeting. Because always I was involved with Hadassah, raising money for Israel and Jewish children, and we had meetings Wednesday nights, each week at another person's house. I was all ready to go, getting on my coat, carrying my plate with the cakes, and he called me over. —Maime, what's that perfume you're wearing?

—Perfume? Oh, I don't know. It's the one I got at the bazaar sale, nothing new.

—I don't remember it. I like it, it smells nice.

I stared at him. He looked back at me from the couch, not saying nothing more. Then he frowned. —Well, go, go, you'll be late for your meeting. What do you think, I can't take care of myself here for a few hours? Turn on the television, please, when you pass.

Then another time, he asked me to make him some rugelach. Somebody was bringing a chocolate rugelach from the bakery to the house and he threw it out, he said it tastes like rubber. —You make the only good rugelach, he told me.

—You never said you like my rugelach.

—So now I'm saying.

—I wish you told me, I would have made it more often. It's my mother's recipe.

There are some people what are helpless in the kitchen, they can't make a simple cake. I go to the supermarket, I see they have some kind of powder, you mix things in and it comes a cake. Berta told me once she bought a cherry pie in a box but then she saw on the directions you have to put it in the oven for fifty minutes so she threw it away. —I don't bake, she said. —This isn't baking, I told her but she don't understand. Well, I'm from a different kind of world. American people talk I like to cook, I don't like to cook, but I never consider myself do I like it. It's just something I do. I don't have no recipe, I just know. My mother also that's how she maked everything.

It was in Poland some days after they took away the store. I came back to the house and she was standing in the kitchen, staring down into a bowl. There was a mound of flour in the bowl and some eggs. When she saw me she looked up and she smiled. —Oh, it's good you're here, she said. —I'm making the pinwheel cookies you like but I can't find the butter. Where do you have the butter?

MARISA KANTOR STARK

—There is no butter, Momma. No sugar either.

—No sugar?

—No.

—What happened to the sugar? I need sugar. What kind of house are you keeping here?

She shook her head. —My own daughter, it's an embarrassment. Not to know even how to keep a house. I notice you got rid of the quilts I gave you.

Something came up in me then, fast and hot. —What's happened to you, Momma? I don't understand it. You're living here in your own little world. Don't you see anything that's happening around you?

She looked at me like she don't recognize me, don't hear what I'm saying. —So the eggs will go to waste. If you don't find some butter there'll be three wasted eggs.

I grabbed the bowl, dumped the eggs and flour into the garbage. —Curse the eggs. Curse you, Momma.

I wasn't thinking to say this, it was like I can't help myself none and the words just came from my mouth. All those months listening to her talk and telling myself to keep quiet, she don't mean what she's saying, it breaked in me that minute.

First she looks surprised, then hurt, but then nothing. Her face is empty. It don't mean nothing to her, she forgot already. So I was thinking to apologize but I was too stubborn, I tell myself what's the difference, she don't know, she don't care. But I wasn't thinking then how I will care. All the years later I care. Because now here it is, the way I talked to her that day and left the room, my anger big and ugly between us, and there isn't nothing I can do to make it right. If my father knew how I was talking, he would look at me different, I know. I wouldn't be the same daughter to him. And even though he wouldn't say, it would be there in his eyes. I'm sorry, Momma, Tate, I didn't mean it. I never meant it should be this way.

35

After my husband got sick we was going finally to Israel. I always wanted to go but he said —No, we have the store and it's a lot of money to go. But when he was sick I decided this is it, we can't wait no longer, and I asked the doctor can we go. He says   Go, it will be good for him, and I know my husband will listen to this so I told him —The doctor said you should go. And we go.

I was terribly worried because he had Parkinson's and what if something should happen, it will be from me. But Gott was good to us and he was better in Israel. He cried when he saw the land.

The plane landed, everybody clapped and some people was singing shalom aleichem. I have a feeling I can't describe, like coming back to something I'd never even been. I had no idea it will be like this. The lady in the seat next to me was wiping her eyes with a tissue and then I turned to my husband and I saw the tears running on his cheeks.

—Maime. What my father wanted more than anything was to see this land before he died. He said this once, it was the end of the seder and I was almost asleep, but there was something in his voice, I can still hear it. L'shana haba, he said, next year in Yerushalayim. Then he never mentioned it again. But all these years, Maime, why didn't I send my father to Israel? I had the money, Gott knows the money I had. He could go, they could both go. Get out of Poland.

—Saul, there's no purpose to talk like this. I don't want to talk now.

—You know, I still don't understand how we did it. As long as I live that's something I'll never know.

A pause. —The more I think, the more I'm sure there was some other way. We could have hid them like I wanted.

People was starting to get up, collect their bags. Outside the windows of the plane the sky was pink, the sun just starting to come up.

—Maime? Maime, say something, will you. Are you listening to me?

His voice was louder now and he didn't move from his seat. Some people was turned to look at us. All over the airplane babies was crying and suddenly I notice the air is stale, I can hardly breathe. I think if I'm not out soon to breathe some air I will die. I was so tired, my head pounding.

—Saul, I don't want to have this discussion. We had no sleep in thirty-six hours.

He grabbed my arm. —You can say something at least. You don't have to act like you had nothing to do with it. Bringing them.

I pull away. —Don't touch me. I have nothing to say.

I start very fast down the aisle, pushing through the people to the stewardess standing by the exit. It was the same stewardess what brought us meals, drinks, a flat paper pillow and blanket during the flight. She smiled at me like she never had a headache a day in her life. —I hope you and your husband enjoyed your flight.

—Yes, yes it was very nice.

Just get me out from here.

❈ ❈ ❈

There was no tears.

—Tate. Good-bye, Tate. You take care of yourself now, take care of Momma. Until after the war.

My father took my hand. His palm was rough against mine. —Be strong, Maimela. Remember the Jewish people have always been strong.

His eyes holding me there. They was shining with a very bright light, tears maybe that cannot fall. But to me it was like he was seeing something we can't the rest of us see.

Then suddenly I see myself dancing again at my wedding in my father's arms. I hear the fiddle music playing all around us. But something there's wrong. It's too fast like a runaway horse and my father to keep up spins me faster and faster. I'm dizzy, the earth spinning in broken pieces. Now I am falling. My father's hand goes tight over mine and the music stops. I'm still looking up at him.

—Itzak, Maime, are you coming? Hurry, we're leaving.

My mother's voice breaks in. She thinks I'm going with them, she thinks we're all going home. I pull back from my father, turn away. I hear his footsteps against the dirt, the suitcase hitting against his leg. He hurries to the truck.

Over and over I have the same dream. In the dream I'm a little girl and my mother is coming home from America. She has a big doll with a pink dress and she holds it out. —Maimela, look what I brought for you. I reach for the doll and she looks into my face. —Who are you, you're not Maimela. You're not my daughter, where is my daughter? She moves away so I'm looking at her back, the knot of red hair on top her head. It's falling down, I want to go to her and fix it but I cannot. There is a glass door sliding shut between us.

Someplace what I can't see a dog is crying.

The first thing we do in Israel, before we go to the hotel even, we go to the Kotel. This is what we agreed from the beginning, we'll get a taxi to the Kotel and daven there, say Kaddish for our parents. I left my husband and went to the women's place, close up to touch the wall. All around me women was praying, their hands over their face, soft words coming between their fingers. I put my fingers in the cracks. There are hundreds, thousands of notes there, pieces of paper like cement between the stones. People asking things from Gott, each one leaving a question, a prayer, a little piece of their heart. It is the soul of the Jewish people what is inside those stones.

From the Kotel I see the top of a very beautiful building, a gold dome showing the sun like a torch. I asked somebody —What's that building above us? and she told me it is the Dome of the Rock where the Muslims pray. —That rock, she said —that the mosque is built on, is where they say Abraham brought his son Isaac to be sacrificed.

　　　　　　　　　　MARISA KANTOR STARK

The story is come rushing back to me. It was here it happened, here Yitzchak gave his neck open to his father. I never imagined a place like this, in my head it was always a square gray stone like the size of a table, covered over with mosses and circled around with crooked trees.

And Yitzchak kneels, throws his head so his hair is loose across the rock. His eyes glowing with the thing he will do. Avraham looks down for the last time at his son. His heart is empty inside him. All the love and hate in the world coming together to nothing.

Then suddenly the angel, reaching out from the heaven to stop his hand.

I throw back my head. The sky is blue.

I took a scrap of paper to write my own message in the wall. My hand waits there over the paper. You can ask anything, they say, this is the closest touch you can have with Gott. Tell me, Gott, why do you make such a test. This is what I want to ask and I'm thinking to write it, I move my hand to write it. It's what I will always want to know. But then when I look down at the paper I see it's not that, it's a different question what I wrote there. In Jewish I wrote it. Tell me, Gott, was there another way. Something maybe I could have done.

One afternoon we went to kever Rachel, the tomb of Rachel. This is another holy place, women are coming from all over the world to daven for children. There's an old bent woman who stays there, hobbling back and forth to the people. She has a black skirt to the floor and a black kerchief on her head and she keeps a handful of thin red string what she'll give you to tie around your wrist. So she was coming over to me, put her hand like a claw on my arm. —You understand Jewish? I nod and try to pull my arm.

—It really works, you know. I can tell you so many stories. One woman, she came all the way from India, thirteen years she had no children. I give her the string and a brocha, the next year she has a son. Only a shekel I ask, what's one shekel? You can give it to your daughter, she should be, like they say, full with fruit.

—I don't have a daughter. I don't have children.

—Well, then. Now I see, it's you that needs. I can give it to you, it's not too late. You think you're too old, I know, but you're never too old. Gott works in miracles. Sarah, she had Yitzchak born to her when she was ninety years old.

I pulled my arm away.—It wasn't me, I can have children with any man. It was my husband.

She followed after me, holding out the string. —Don't laugh at it, lady, don't laugh. Remember Sarah also laughed and look what Gott did for her. A beautiful son. It's only one shekel.

36

Other people have children. Once Lillian's son came to lunch. Lillian is sitting at my table so she introduced him. —This is my middle son, Stephen, he's a stockbroker. He was bald, his head was pink and shiny like they was polishing it with the floor wax they use in the dining room. On his little finger he had a ring with a square red stone what was flashing when he moved his hand. They sat there across from me at the table. They got their lunch on the green plastic tray.

—This is very nice, Mother. Look at all these friends you have.

—What?

—I said it's nice.

—Oh, nice. Yes.

He turned to me. —So you're Maime. I heard a lot about you.

—What? What you heard?

—Oh, all nice things, you can be sure. Hey, this is a real lunch they give you. Better than I get at home. That's some pear you've got there, Mother.

I look at Lillian's pear. It's in wax paper but I see it has a bruise by the stem. A brown mark shaped like a heart, spreading like a cap over the top of the fruit. Anybody with eyes can see it and know in another day that pear will be rotten. I decide I don't like Lillian's son.

❋   ❋   ❋

They had here a Mother's Day brunch. It was a party with bagels, coffee, a little bit of lox. I wasn't hungry. I took some, I eat because I have to eat and it's kosher, but I was never a big eater. During the war, after the war, I was never hungry and now when it comes Yom Kippur I could fast another whole day, it wouldn't bother me. Karyn says to me —What's the matter, don't you like it? so I tell her it's too salty.

The women what usually sit at my table weren't there. Lillian was with her son, he came and took her someplace in a big white car. And Berta had visitors, her son and one of her daughters and some grandchildren, so they was going together to a different table.

—Maime, you want to sit with us? I can move the walker, we'll bring another chair.

—No, thank you. I'll stay here.

I'm not going to impose myself there to their party. Anyway another friend was still at the table, I wasn't completely alone. She can't speak but she is some company, it's better than nobody.

My nephew was thinking to be coming but he had something to do, he was away. Well, you know, I don't blame him. He's a busy man, he has a wife and family, even grandchildren. They live their life, I live mine. In the summer every year he goes to some islands on a cruise. A few times he asked me will

MARISA KANTOR STARK

I come but I say no because I know it's a lot of money and it is his life. I don't ask from him to give me nothing. I know he don't really want me there, a woman past ninety. But he has to ask me they should think what a wonderful nephew.

They had different tablecloths, pink and white, and a rose in the middle of each table. Some children was coming from a school to sing. They both was American children but they was singing a few songs in Hebrew what I recognize, a lady was playing them on the piano. Then a woman here I know, Doris, she grabbed my hand. —Come on you, let's dance, dance, dance. Wheee. She's crazy, that Doris. She can't hardly walk even and she's thinking to dance.

The children were lined up in a line in front of the room. There was one little girl what had a white dress and braids with white ribbons on the end, I was watching her more than the others. Because she was standing closest to my table, I could see her face, and I saw she's patchking with something in her mouth, a tooth it looked. She had a tissue rolled in her hand and between the songs she was sticking it in her mouth and when she takes it away there's dots of blood. She tried to hide it in her hand.

I remember the first time my tooth fell out I was seven years old. My father said leave it under the pillow and I wrap it in a handkerchief and tuck it there when I go to sleep. Then in the morning I stick my hand under and feel the handkerchief and there's something bigger inside, a silver coin. I asked my father did he put it there and my grandfather says —No, it was the stork.

After the singing they gave to all the women a flower, not a real one but a tissue flower with paper leaves. The girl gave me the yellow one and I kissed her. —Thank you, dear, have a good yur. Then I open my purse and found for her a fresh tissue. —Here, take this with you. You know, you shouldn't play so much with your tooth. When it's ready to come out it will come.

I used to have braids like that.

The flower smelled like some kind of perfume. It reminded me from the magazines they have in the library what you open them and they put such a strong scent I have to sneeze. I put it on top of my dresser but later I had to throw it away.

Those children said they will come again but they don't come. I know it's my nephew, he chased them away. He don't want I should have friends, he told them not to come no more.

In Poland there was no Mother's Day. To us every day was mother's day. I remember my father always saying to me and my brother —Help your momma, she works hard. Don't forget to tell her how good is the food she made. And every Friday night after he said Kiddush we used to sing to her where she was sitting there at one head of the table. Eishet chayil, a woman of valor.

37

Lunch here is at 11:30. My watch is no good, I don't know the time, but some days I come early to help the lady. She puts down the tablecloths then I help her to put out the bibs. I take them very carefully from the box, they shouldn't rip, because they're only paper, white with a plastic string what ties around the neck, and when they're finished they throw them away. The first time I saw them I said —There's no way I'm wearing such a bib. But then one time my hand was shaking and I spilled the pea soup and they said —You see, Maime, you need to wear it. What can I say, I don't want to ruin my dress. You know, I don't have that many clothes, I try to keep them decent.

Yesterday I came to help and she said —I don't need help today, I'm in a hurry. So I see I'm in the way, she don't need me no more, and if she don't want she don't want. I go over, sit on the chair by my table. It smells like green beans, they're cooking them too long again. The green beans here are always gray.

—Maime, it's only 10:30. Why don't you go for a walk or something?

—I don't feel like having a walk. I'll sit here, don't bother about me.

I watched her put out the bibs, one folded white square neatly to each place.

I always liked to walk. I have good shoes for it with laces and thick rubber soles. When it's warm I take a little sweater and go outside. In the front is the awning, green and white stripes, with two benches and some plastic white tables in the sun. Also there's the sign, a big sign shaped like a tree what holds the letters, hanging by the door. To me this sign is the place. It reminds me everything, and if I'm thinking where am I, how did I come here and then I see it, so I know.

And there's some white flowers. I don't know who planted them, I think they grow by themselves in the row against the building, but they're very pretty. Flowers are making anything look a little bit nice.

Until today I thought there was no place to walk really, just up by the parking lot and back. All around is busy streets, stores, traffic lights, different houses and apartments. It's terribly dangerous, they said, not a place for older people, and I believe them. So I'd go up just a little bit on the sidewalk then turn around. That's all, it never came to me to try nothing else.

But I have to be very careful. Because one time I was walking on the sidewalk here by the building and a man drove up in a car asking me —Do you want a ride? I said no and I

MARISA KANTOR STARK

turned around and walked back very fast. And then another time the car was coming and he was asking. So I have to be terribly careful where I'm walking. They can come and take you away. Put you someplace you're never coming out.

I had a band they shouldn't lose me. It was going around my wrist, it said Maime Schatz, Edgewood Manor, and also the medicine what I'm taking. Because they are forgetful, they forget to give me the medicine. Then I get terrible headaches, I have to go to the desk in the front and remind them. —You forgot my medicine again.

—Maime, you had it at lunch. See, you signed here that you had.

—Where? Let me see.

—Right here.

She shows me a card. I didn't sign that, it's not my writing. It's too shaky. The nurses and doctors, they don't know nothing.

During the war we had yellow arm bands. But before we left we burned them. I mean we tried to burn them, I couldn't make it to light. I stood over the stove with a match, striking one after the other, watching the edge of the cloth curl and turn to black before the flames go out. There was the dry smell of burning cloth. My husband came up behind me, looks over my shoulder. —Just leave it, Maime. Leibish is waiting for us.

—No, let me try something else.

I wrapped the yellow cloth in some old rags a different material, maybe it's the material, they make it so it can't burn. I touched the flame to the rags and the fire jumped. But when it was gone down I see the pieces from the armbands are still there, curled up in the ashes.

—I don't understand why it won't burn.

—I don't know. There's no more time.

We covered it with the ashes, closed the stove. Then we slipped out the back door into the night.

38

—Maime!

It was the week before he died, my husband waked me in the night. He was sitting straight up in the bed, his face flushed, the hair sticking wet on his forehead. The blankets was twisted in knots around his legs. I sit up to face him.

He pointed at me, his finger shaking. —You, Maime. I blame you. Do you hear me, I blame you for everything.

—Saul, what is this? What are you talking about?

—I said to hide them. All along that's what I said. You know that, don't you, I wanted to hide them? You always knew that.

He tries to keep his finger there, pointing at my face, but he can't and his arm is swinging wildly back and forth, now to the window, now to the door. His shoulders, his head, his whole body is shaking. I'm thinking to grab him, hold him still, but I don't move.

Finally he dropped back against the pillow. He was breathing funny, for a long time there will be nothing, like he's holding his breath, then suddenly a gasp for air. I listen and my mind is nothing except that, waiting for another breath. Whenever he was quiet I thought this is it, he won't breathe now again, but then it was come. I read once where a person can't hold their breath long enough to die. No matter how hard you try, you start to breathe.

I sat at the edge of the bed, staring into the dark. I didn't feel at all my body, it was like I was spread out and floating over the room. Only my hands I felt, resting like stones in my lap. My wedding ring shined.

A small, dry cough. —Maime, are you there?

I don't answer him. The dark is wrapped around me, pulling me back there. Poland, a different bedroom, another night. A part of me is always there. It don't matter what I'm doing if I'm here in this country and with people or what. It's never all of me. You shouldn't think it's all of me you see here.

MARISA KANTOR STARK

39

My wedding ring I gave to my nephew. It was a nice ring but I won this other one in bingo and the only place it fits is my wedding finger. It's so pretty with this big green stone, it's a shame not to be wearing it. Berta said —You can give it to me, it fits on my little finger no problem. But I say —No, I want to keep it. So I'm wearing it on my wedding finger and the other I give to my nephew. He can do with it whatever, I'm sure he'll think of something.

There's a couple here what they was married together sixty-two years. Their name is Florence and Al and they have a room in the east wing with one big bed with a yellow bedspread and no other people. I know because once I looked inside.

Florence is sick, she takes a medicine what makes her always very tired. She sits in her wheelchair with her eyes closed like she's not listening but she can hear and really she is listening. She talks very slow so you have to wait a long time if she will answer.

He never leaves her, they're always together. Every day he comes to the nurse. —Is it a nice day, can I take my wife outside? And if she says yes it's all right then he will go. First he gets her sweater with the wooden buttons and puts it around her shoulders. Then he pushes her up and down in front of the building, sometimes when I'm walking I pass them and he nods at me. He talks very quietly to her, I can't never hear what he's saying.

One day I see she's dressed very nice. Under the sweater she has a blue dress with white dots and a gold pin like a flower on top by the collar.

—Florence, you're so nice, what's the occasion?

She don't answer me. Al leaned over the back of the chair. —It's our anniversary, isn't that right, dear? Do you know how many years we're married? Tell Maime how many years.

For a long time she don't say nothing and I think she isn't going to answer. I smile, start to move away, but then very slow and quiet without opening her eyes she answers. —Sixty . . . two . . . years.

—That's right. Sixty-two wonderful years.

He looks at me but I can tell it's not me he is seeing. There's something else, his eye is wet at the corner and a little smile on his mouth. So it's him too what has another place and the others also it must be they have. But for them it must be like a nice dream what they carry from the night into the day and makes them warm and safe to think on it.

For me it's every way different.

MARISA KANTOR STARK

❈ ❈ ❈

Florence has a doll she keeps on her lap. It's a rag doll with black buttons for eyes and orange hair and red freckles across the nose. A blue cotton dress with a pocket. So one time they passed by, I saw my nephew looking at her.

—You think it's funny, Milton, she has a doll?

—What? Oh, no, I was just . . .

—Well, I'll tell you, it's not so funny. She's like a child. Old people, you know, they can be like children.

❈ ❈ ❈

I always liked dolls. Those applehead dolls what I maked with my sister, when I got married and moved in with my in-laws so I took them with me. There was five of them, three women, two men. My mother-in-law looked at them and she said —Dolls, Maime, what do you need, soon you'll have children, but then she said —Well, it's nice, maybe you'll have a daughter. You can give them to her.

I put the dolls on a shelf in my room. Each one had their own special place and a name because when I was young I gave them names. It was a game me and Raisa was playing to think of all the names we liked and don't like and say what names we'll call our children. I remember Raisa liked the name Simeon but I thought that's an awful name. I will never name my child Simeon.

Later when I moved with my husband to the town I still had those dolls and I packed them up to bring them. They was terribly old, they had skin like brown leather and little cracks in the cheeks and around the eyes. But to me they were like dear, familiar friends.

But then something happened to them. I don't know were they getting wet or what but suddenly they started to go rotten. My husband noticed. —Maime, those dolls are smelling up the room, and he was right, I had to get rid of them. I hated to do it, to throw away like that such a piece from my childhood, but there wasn't no choice, there wasn't nothing else I could do. It turned my heart. To see them lying dead on top the pile of garbage.

40

He sent in two Gentile girls to give me pills. It was early in the morning, half past six they woke me up, and it wasn't Karyn, it was two other girls. They was standing by the door, I should take these white pills. I said —No, my nurse brings me the pills with my breakfast, I have to sign. But they said —Here are the pills, take them.

Well, I can't fight, they was bigger than me and two of them. So I took the pill and I put it in my cheek. Then I was making like to cough and I said —I don't have no water, and I turned to the side and put it in my hand. When they wasn't looking I threw it to the garbage. They ran away. I came to the desk and they know they're in trouble so they ran away.

This is something from him, from my nephew. I was telling him about it and now they don't come no more so I know it was him what was sending them. If once more they're going to come, I'm going to scream for help.

He had another aunt what she was very rich. She didn't have no children and she was staying by him the same time I was staying there. She had a room near mine, we shared the bathroom with the pink bathtub, and I helped to give her a bath. Because she was an older woman, she couldn't do for herself, and if I didn't bathe her nobody will do it, they'll let her to go dirty. But always she was a strong woman, she ate like a man what worked on a railroad.

One day he told me —She'll have her breakfast early, I'm taking her to the office. This was when he was still working as a doctor, before he was retired. I said —What she's going to do in your office? and he says —She'll sit and talk to me. So I gave her breakfast, such an appetite she had, she ate a breakfast like two mans. Then he took her to his office. He gave her lunch there.

In the afternoon he called the house. —Tanta Anna passed away. Just like that. —Tanta Anna passed away. I asked him what happened and he said —Nothing happened, she just passed away sitting in the chair. Then he made to talk of something else.

Well, I know he poisoned her. She was a strong woman, I used to talk to her and not even from one little finger she didn't complain. I can talk this to anyone, to a lawyer, a rabbi, anyone who will listen. She had two other nephews but they wasn't so smart like him. She had an awful lot of money and he took it all.

❋ ❋ ❋

Once I was thinking I can get a lawyer. There was a woman here to make a rummage sale, she has skirts and dresses hanging

MARISA KANTOR STARK

on metal racks with wheels in the dayroom. —Can I get you something? she asks me. —We have some nice skirts.

She shows me a blue skirt and I pull it over my clothes.

—I can use some things. I'll take this skirt. But I have nothing to pay you.

—Oh, don't worry about that. We'll charge it to your account. It'll all be taken care of later.

I look at her. She looks a nice lady. And what's most important she's from the outside, she don't know my nephew, she can't tell him nothing. I come close to her, put my hand on her arm. —Can you help me? I say in a very soft whisper.

—Are you having trouble getting it off? Here, let me . . .

—No, not the skirt. I need a lawyer.

—A lawyer?

—Yes, a lawyer. You know what's a lawyer?

—Why do you need a lawyer?

—It's too much time to explain. But I need. Will you get me one?

She takes a step back. She's not looking at me, her eyes is moving around the room like she's looking for somebody else.

—Listen, hon, this is a fundraiser. I'm with the volunteer fire agency. I don't know anything about lawyers.

She takes the skirt from me and starts to walk away. I watch her back. There is a yellow stain on her shirt by the collar. I hate for people to call me hon.

—My name is Maime, I call after her.

My husband is buried near here someplace. It's on a hill, Milton bought for us a piece of land. It's a very windy place, I remember from the funeral I was wearing a scarf on my head and it kept blowing off, Milton had to go after it. It was autumn. I don't remember too much from the funeral, Milton handled everything. Just they said —Maime, throw a handful of dirt, and I bent down and grabbed in my fingers the cold black earth and I threw it on my husband's grave. And I watched it fall I'm thinking now this is it, I'm the only one left.

After a year I was gone back to say Kaddish by the grave. I'm thinking how he used to hold my elbow when we walked together and bend his head a little. In the morning he liked egg toasts made from challah with sprinkled sugar and salt. He could finish the whole challah that way.

Then I see the stone is in place, my nephew had it made. And I see there's a place for me there next to my husband. My nephew was talking to us about it once in the apartment when my husband was still alive, to have a family plot and such, but I forgot until that day I see one side carved with my husband's name, Saul Schatz, and the other side empty. Smooth gray marble.

It gave me a twist in my stomach to see it, to think this is where I will be. Because to think what it is to be dead is like trying to remember before you was born and when I look at the ground I can't help to wonder what it's like to be there and to feel nothing, remember nothing. What I remember is all what I am. But I'm glad to have this place and rub the dirt between my fingers. It's a comfort to have such a place.

For my parents, they should rest in peace, there wasn't no such place. Poland, you know, is the biggest cemetery. But there are no graves.

MARISA KANTOR STARK

41

How he can say it was from me. I thought it over and over again, I never stop thinking, and I know there was no way we could hide them.

We was all together in my in-laws' house, me, my husband, my parents and my husband's parents. It was too many people to live in such a small place, it starts to get on people's nerves. And especially they say parents and in-laws it's hard living together.

My father was walking up and down the room from the window to the wall and back to the window. He was a bare man now, his land, his books, nothing was left to him. —Are you looking for something? my father-in-law asked him.

—Just thinking.

—I don't know what there is to think so much, my mother-in-law says. —It doesn't change things.

—Do you have some books, maybe, I can read?

—Books? No. What would we have with books?

My mother watched them from the chair, her eyes moving back and forth to this one's face what's talking. It was my father-in-law's chair by the fire, it was the only place in the house what she liked to sit. We had to bring even her meals to her there in that chair. At night when my father-in-law was coming home my mother-in-law said —That's my husband's chair you're sitting in, Ruth. Maybe you'll move to another place?

—No, let her stay there, my father-in-law said. He brought a wooden chair from the kitchen and put it to the other side of the fire. —I can sit here.

She kept a plaid blanket around her, she was always cold. Every day she asked my father when we're going home. —Well, I'm ready, Itzak. Enough visit, I think we should be going.

—We can't go home, Ruth. Not yet.

—Why? Why can't I go home?

—It's a war.

—I thought the war is over.

—No, it's not over.

—Well, when will it be over? Tell me when.

—I cannot tell you. I am sorry, Ruthie. I'm so very sorry.

We all wanted to believe it will be soon, we tried the best we know to go on with our life. My father-in-law kept working, going around to the farmers to check their eggs. He wasn't well, he had an awful cough what was getting worse and worse and it wasn't easy for him to breathe. From smoking tobacco, the dust filled up inside his lungs.

My mother-in-law said —What do you need this for, Yusef, the farmers don't need an egg candler. Because they couldn't sell their eggs no more to the stores, they don't buy from Jewish people. But still he would go, every morning waking up before it was light and harnessing the horses to the wagon.

Some days my husband went with him. The farmers couldn't pay him nothing but they give him from the eggs. My mother-in-law boiled them, chopped them into something we should eat. Chopped eggs with salt on a piece of bread.

—So it's a war, we still have to eat, she said every night when she put the dishes on the table. We come together at the table, put the radio between us. There was not much talk, we ate our food and listened for the news. German troops enter Stalingrad. —Turn the volume, Yusef, I can't hear what they're saying. Static. We leaned our elbows on the table. Forces surrender. —Did you know, they burned the yeshiva in Lublin, the great yeshiva. I heard today in the village. And they're destroying the cemeteries.

My father's mouth goes hard. I know he is thinking of my brother's grave. All the years he was keeping it, going each week before Shabbos to pull the weeds. When they moved to us in the town he can't go as often, but still my husband would take him in the wagon. But now no. From my in-laws' village it's too far and Jewish people aren't traveling.

After supper we played cards, drank coffee bitter without sugar. —You know what I want more than anything? my mother-in-law said. —I want some chocolate. First thing after the war, I'm going to have a cup of hot chocolate with heavy cream.

Yes. I can feel the sweetness on my tongue.

One day my husband decides to fix the roof. It was getting old he said and he took some tools in a bag. —In a few years it won't be any good.

It was Shabbos afternoon, about two o'clock, they were gone out for a walk. Every week this was the time people come out, gathered together in the streets. But I stayed in the house with my mother. Somebody has to stay and on that day I don't feel like to be seeing people.

When I came into the kitchen I was surprised to see my father sitting at the table, wrapped in his tallis. His eyes was closed, he was saying tehillim.

—Tate.

With his hand he tells me to be quiet. I poured some coffee and sat down across him at the table. He opened his eyes.

—Tate, what are you doing here? I thought you went out.

—No, I didn't want. I wanted to talk to you.

—What is it?

—Maime, I want you to listen to me. You and Saul must go away.

—Go where, Tate?

—Anywhere, any place but here. Before it's too late.

I don't want to hear like this what he's saying. I stirred the coffee, spinning circles around in the cup. Closing in smaller and smaller.

—There's no place to go, Tate. They aren't letting the Jews leave Poland anymore.

—There are ways. You have money, you can find a way.

—Come, Tate, this is silly. You know we aren't going to leave you.

—No, that's how you're wrong. A long time I've been thinking about this and I know you're wrong. You must leave. Everybody has a test in life. For you will be the test to survive.

—Tate, please don't talk like that. This is a bad time, it won't be forever.

—No, Maimela. Your mother and me, we had our life. But you are young, you and Saul.

—Not so young, Tate. Look at me, I'm not a young woman anymore.

—I want you to promise me.

—Promise what?

—Whatever you have to do, you do. I want you to survive.

❖ ❖ ❖

There was rumors. In the streets, in the houses, people talking. We told each other they can't be true. —Crazy stories, my mother-in-law said. —Exaggerations. This is not a jungle we're living in, this is Poland. Four generations my family lived in this country, in this village.

My father shook his head. —I don't know, Gussie. I just don't know.

—Suppose they are true, people said. —What will we do when they come here, to this our village? There was talk to run, hide, go into the woods. —But the children, they said. —What can we do with the children? And the old people, what about them?

I lie awake in the bed next to my husband. I can't erase from my mind my father's words. There is fear like a black thing growing all the time inside me. It was a fear the way I never know before this or after, not even when finally it came. Because I did then what I had to do and that was all. The roar of the engine, wheels of the trucks making dirt into dust. It's over, what meaning is there to be afraid. It was only now I was afraid.

I wanted with a fierce hardness to survive.

❖ ❖ ❖

It was night. The room was dark, only one candle burning on the table in the corner. It was a room I know, the room my husband brought me the first night we're married and I moved to this house. There's the same low ceiling, the same two beds what my husband pushed together to make one bed. I was young then, just a girl really, I didn't know nothing to be with a man. What things I was wondering about, not knowing how it will be, and I remember thinking my in-laws' room is so close next door, the walls are so terribly thin.

It feels now like a different life, some other people's life. Me and my husband on the separate beds, leaning to each other in the dark. And the same like it was then, I'm thinking will they hear us, or my parents, what were sleeping on a cot in the kitchen, will hear. —Quiet, stay quiet, I tell him.

His voice is a hot whisper. —Maime, Leibish wants us to hide with him. He has a place. They came to his village, shot his family.

—The whole family? But what about the children? Oh, Gott, no, please don't say the children.

—Yes. We're next, Maime. We have to go with him.

He stops talking, waits for what I will say. But he knows already, there can be only this one thing to say.

—Our parents, Saul. We have our parents.

He was waiting I should be the one to give it words.

—We'll bring them with us, he says.

I laughed and not because it is funny. It's because it is not funny I laughed.

—Tell me, Saul, how are we going to feed so many people? How will we hide your father with his cough and my mother who's like a little child? Tell me that, I'm waiting to hear.

He has no answer. I don't expect he'll have an answer. Because he is a coward, he's thinking he can say these things, say

MARISA KANTOR STARK

we will hide them, and that's all, now whatever happens is from me.

And later he can say it was me.

42

After the war it was Milton what brought us to this country.

We ran away from Poland and came to Germany. When we was come out from hiding so we can't stay there in that country, the Polish people will kill us and we had nothing, not the house, not the store. All what we had is gone, everything the Hitlers are taking. In Germany there's camps for such people what was left over from the war, the Americans maked what they called it the UNRRA. We went to Bergen-Belsen.

In the camp people wanted to go to America. If you had someone, anyone, an old friend or a second cousin, you tried to make a correspondence. For my sister Lia I didn't have an address. I don't know what happened to her letters. Only later when we got to America I found her again. But I had an address of my nephew. I never met him but the address I had. When we got married he sent to my husband a letter, and my husband saved it in the attic. Then after the war he was going back to the house to get it. Other people were living there, Gentiles, but they let him to go in the attic and get the address. —Go quickly, we won't stop you. Not all of them hated the Jews, there are all kinds of people in Poland.

I took that address with me to Bergen-Belsen and I had it there on a piece of paper. There was American soldiers coming with food, supplies, and such. Different kinds of medicine. So I stopped one and I said —Please will you take for me a letter. I was very stubborn he should listen to me, I stand myself in front of him so he can't pass until he heard. I'm speaking only Polish and Jewish and he was speaking English but I maked him to understand.

Then I told him —Wait, don't move, and I ran back to the room where we was staying. It was a barrack, during the war it was a camp. I wrote down quickly on a paper, We are here, we're alive, and I put that paper in the envelope with the address. I give the envelope to the soldier. But then I realize I don't have a stamp and I was frantic where can I get a stamp. When he saw what's the problem he says not to worry, he'll buy the stamp and mail it for me in America. My heart was full. —Gott bless you, you have a mitzvah from Gott.

Then we wait.

The camp was many, many people and all of them waiting. They was waiting to hear who is alive, who survived the war, and they move from camp to camp looking for a mother, a cousin, even a fourth cousin. Leibish was with us for a little while then he left to look for his brother's family. But I told my husband —We're not leaving. We have to stay here, so he'll know where to find us. Otherwise how he will know?

It was almost two months and my husband says he isn't coming. —We should move on, Maime. Maybe there is somebody, one of my sister's children. It must be some of them survived. Or your mother's brother's family. It was far away, who can say what happened to them there?

—No, Saul. We're not leaving.

—How long are we going to wait here?

—Until we hear something.

—You're crazy. I'm not waiting very much longer.

—You go then. I will wait.

Finally we got a telegraph. It was my husband's nephew, Milton, he was in the army in Vienna and I didn't know and now he is coming. —See, Saul what did I tell you. Someone from the family is coming for us.

The other people knew we were waiting and some boys maked with us teasing. One day we were walking, me and my husband, and they said —Maime, Saul, you better hurry back, your nephew is here. We ran back to the house. You know, we wasn't strong, not hungry really, we had plenty food in the camp, but we wasn't so strong to be running like that. And then there wasn't nobody there. They thought this is funny, they was making fun, but it's not fun. It was a terrible cruel thing what they were doing, Gott should punish.

So another time they're saying again —Hurry, your nephew is here, and this time we don't run. I said —You go back there and tell him to wait for us. And we continue walking slow, slow the way we're doing.

But then one night we were eating supper and there was a knock at the door and it was a different knock. When I open it was standing there two soldiers with American hats. The one steps up to me, past me to my husband. —Is dus Saul Schatz? He was talking like that in Jewish. My husband knew him because he looked like my husband, big and dark with thick

MARISA KANTOR STARK

black hair, and he says to me —This is him, Maime, this is the one. He's one from my family.

He was come with a truck, an ambulance, and so much food. —I thought you would be starving.

—We're not starving. We have what we need.

—I'm sorry it took me this long. My wife, Debbie, she sent a telegraph you were here but I couldn't come right away. We get leave only for parents or grandparents. I told them you were my grandparents but still I had to wait. Is there . . . was there nobody else?

—Nobody what we know from.

For three days he stayed there, we should get ready to go. He was thinking to sleep in the ambulance with the other soldier but this I won't allow. —No, you sleep inside with us. We had there one stove, a small black-belly stove for keeping warm and doing a little bit of cooking. There was already ten people in the room and there wasn't enough beds, they were sleeping with blankets on the floor. But I found for him a bed near the stove, sleeping with my husband, and I take a blanket for myself on the floor. He should have the best what we can give.

Because at that time I thought different about him. I didn't know then what he was.

The house in Poland is still there, not in the village but the one in town what my husband built. My nephew was gone after the war with his wife, he said it's important to him to go there. It's another people's house now, a Gentile family. There's not too many Jews left in Poland. Some, I have a friend, but not too many. So he took photographs of the house and he brought them to me. I have them here in my room. It was such a beautiful house.

People are asking me would I ever go back to Poland. I tell them —No, why should I go back, there's nothing there for me no more. Now I'm in a good country, in Gott's country. And it's quiet here, there are no wars. In Europe one after the other there is wars.

But even so I don't hate nobody. One time in the apartment Lou saw I have something, some chachka what's made in Germany, and she says —How can you buy that, look where it's made. So I told her —Thank Gott I'm not left with no hatred, I don't hate the German people or the Polish people. It was a Polish man what was hiding us during the war and he was a goy, a Gentile.

When my nephew came back he maked some kind of scrap-book with the pictures. He brought it to the apartment, I remember we was sitting together on the sofa and he showed it to me. A heavy book with a leather cover.

—Yes, that's it. That's the house. Would you believe, it looks exactly the same. That was my window in front, on the side here is my parents' window. You know, first my husband wanted to have his parents with us there in the house but I said no, I wanted my own parents.

—Uh huh, you've told me that, Tanta.

—I had a reason. I mean they were my parents, I have to take care of them. I promised my sister I'll take care of them.

—Well, you were a good daughter to them. You certainly did everything you could.

—No. No, Milton, I did not. I had to bring them, did I tell you? Did I ever tell you what I did, how I was bringing them?

—Yes, you told me.

—When? When I told you?

—A lot. Every time I see you, practically. What can I say? It was a terrible thing.

I stare closely at the pictures. Now I see there's a face at one of the windows what I didn't notice it before.

—Who's this?

He smiles. —Oh, that's the woman that lives there. She was watching me from the window while I took the pictures. I'm not sure she trusted me.

I put the page up to my eyes. The face is blurry, I can't see it too good. I can't see what she looks like. I think maybe she has light hair. I feel my nephew looking closely at me. He touches my hand.

—You know, Tanta, I always tell you, you can't blame yourself. All these years . . . you just can't blame yourself. You have to let go.

—Is this all the pictures, Milton? There's no more?

—Nope, that's it. Why? What else were you expecting?

I close the book.

—Nothing. I don't know. I just thought maybe there's one I missed.

43

It was a Tuesday morning in August, three days after Leibish first came to the village. It was hot. I smell the heat in the air, feel it pressing to my tongue. Little pieces of hair stick to my neck. The kind of day you wake up tired, wishing already it to be over.

The trucks arrived in the middle morning. Even before we saw them we knew they were coming, felt the shiver in the ground. It was a relief almost, I couldn't stand no more this waiting. My husband was gone out to see what will happen.

My mother dozed in the chair by the window, a white shawl around her shoulders. I sat watching her sleep. Her mouth was open, I could see her gold tooth and a wet line dribbled slowly down her chin. My father-in-law sat with me. We don't talk.

In the kitchen my mother-in-law was washing clothes in a wood tub. I heard the hard back and forth of her scrubbing. —Germans or no, we still need what to wear, she said.

A fat black fly buzzed around my mother's lips. I pushed it away. It maked a circle, landed on the back of her chair. I tried

MARISA KANTOR STARK

to hit it with my hand but I missed and it came up like to tease me. I try again. I'll get that fly, I think. All I can think now is I'll get that fly.

I feel my father-in-law's eyes on my hand.

—Maime.

He reached out to me. His hand on my knee. —Don't torture yourself, Maime. Leave it be.

Those are the words I last remember from him. It must be he said something later, when we left, but I don't know. I can't remember.

. . . I'm in the forest, picking berries. It's very hot, my clothes stick to my back. I roll my sleeves past my elbows. Into the basket I drop bright red berries piling them higher and higher. Suddenly a bird comes down and attacks the basket. A black bird, big and terrible, stealing my berries, breaking them open with his beak. I grab the basket tight to my chest and start to run. Look down at my hands. They're stained with red. Wings beating in my ears like pounding feet . . .

Where is Tate? I jump up suddenly. When did I see him, was it at breakfast or after breakfast, I can't think. I run through the rooms of the house. Everything is like always. The curtains are tied, the beds are neat. But my father. Then I hear a noise in the pantry and I go in. He is there, sitting on the bottom of the ladder to the attic. He is polishing his shoes.

—Tate! I couldn't find you. I couldn't find you anywhere. I didn't know where you were.

—It's all right, Maimela. Come.

He holds out his hand to me and I go to him, stand looking down at the top of his head. He rubs the shoes with a cloth until they shine.

❈ ❈ ❈

We go to the door, all except my mother who was still sleeping. German soldiers in black uniforms was running through the village, closing like dark water over the streets. Hats, boots, the black spider on their sleeves. The Einsatzgruppen.

A man with a speaker was shouting from the square. —The children and old people at noon to the square! One suitcase each person! Noon and no later!

Bring us die alt war, zum Schiessen!

❈ ❈ ❈

My husband came home, the door slammed. My mother woke up. —What? What's happening? What's that noise?

Nobody answered her. She looked at my husband.

—And who is this? Who's this strange man in the house?

My father put his hands on her shoulders. Nobody moved.

❈ ❈ ❈

I don't know how much time is passed. Me and my husband was in our room. We're standing between the beds, very close but not touching, my husband is saying again they have a list.

MARISA KANTOR STARK

The names of all the people in the village, how many in each house, what are the relatives, these kind of things. He's talking very fast, the words falling on top of each other from his lips.

—All right, Saul, I hear you. I hear.

—We have to bring them, if not they'll shoot us.

—Yes. We have to bring them.

—You know what we're doing, don't you? You know they'll kill them. I mean, what else, where else would they be taking them?

—I don't know, I have no idea. But they can't kill so many people. It's impossible. Calm yourself, Saul. They're trying to make us afraid.

I can't remember did I believe it then or not. I don't think I believed nothing at all. I didn't feel nothing. It was only my body there, moving like it had to move and saying what it had to say. A body can do anything. But my husband didn't notice how it was. He keeps talking. He didn't never know the woman I really am.

—We should have brought them to hiding. Like I told you. We're going to die anyway, Maime, before it's over. We're all going to die.

I helped my mother pack her suitcase. An extra pair of shoes, a hairbrush.

—Are we going home now, Maimela? Finally. I'm ready to go home.

❊ ❊ ❊

Noon. The sun bright over our heads.

—Ruth Leiber!

—She is here.

—Itzak Leiber!

—Here.

—Yusef and Gittel Schatz!

—Here. Here.

—Where?

—Here.

I stand with my husband. They're lining the people, loading them onto open trucks. Cattle trucks, the men and women together. Children in another. I thank Gott a hundred times I have no children. My father lets go my hand, picks up my mother's suitcase. There are no tears.

—It's just till after the war, Saul, I tell my husband. —It must be that. Older people, they need to be taken care of.

But still I'm standing there, I don't move. I'm waiting for something to happen, for somebody to change their mind. Stop, it is enough. Don't bring your hand against these people. But there is nothing. The smell of hot skin. They're crowding to the trucks.

Suddenly I hear my mother's voice. —Maimela!

Her hand pushes through the bodies, reaching out to me from the truck.

A woman throws herself to a small child, screaming, the soldier pulls her back. Kicks her with his boot to the ground.

I look away.

MARISA KANTOR STARK

❈   ❈   ❈

The clothes are still in the tub in the kitchen. A little piece of soap was melting in the water. On the chair is my mother's shawl.

—Saul, we can't wait here any more. Tell Leibish we will go with him.

I sit by myself in the house. I wrap myself in the shawl.

It is hot. There is a fly buzzing.

She left her shawl. She will be cold.

44

So that's how it was. After the war we looked at the lists. They died at Auschwitz. My parents and my husband's parents, it's written in the book. It don't say there how they died.

I don't think no more it will be so hard to die. That was when I was younger, I thought the hardest thing is to die. But I know now it's not that way. The hardest thing is to survive. The biggest test is to live and every day to keep on living.

MARISA KANTOR STARK

45

I decided not to sit no more and wait for my nephew. Nobody is keeping me here.

I took with me a knife from my breakfast tray, what they use it to spread the jelly, and after I got away from the building I cut off the band from my wrist. I was thinking to burn it but I don't have no match or nothing so I threw it in the garbage can at the end of the parking lot. If they should see me, they'll think I'm just going for another walk, just to the end of the sidewalk and never further. But they don't know nothing.

I held my bag very tight against me. At the first traffic light I came to I waited a long time, because the lights was changing very fast. As soon I was thinking to cross, it was red again, and I kept putting my foot to the street and then taking it back. A car came speeding around the corner and a man shouts at me something from the window. So I was waiting until some people came along I should cross with them.

The city is like a place left over from the war. The houses with broken windows, paint peeling, porches breaking into the ground. At the corner I see a brick building with a worn-out leather boot hanging by one lace from an upstairs window. It was knocking back and forth in the wind, making a noise against the pane. Why should a person hang their boot like that out from a window. Once I saw a lady's gold shoe with a high heel lying on the curb and I was thinking about it for days, how it got there.

There's a garbage can fell over on the sidewalk. Pigeons are walking there, picking the dirty bread crumbs.

My head was starting to hurt, oh, what about my medicine, they forgot again. Maybe I'll take a bus. I found a bus stop and there was a bench. It was orange cracked plastic, such a filthy bench. Bird mess on it and some kind of writing I don't recognize from no place across the seat and along the back. It's so dirty, I can't sit on this. I took a tissue from my bag and wiped the seat before I sat down.

I don't know how long and then a lady sat down next to me. I didn't see her coming but all of a sudden she was there, a very big black woman with a white turban tied around her head, and when she sits down it's with a noise like it was hard for her. So she looks at me and her eyes moved to my dress, my bag, and I know she's looking for the band around my wrist.

—I don't need that no more, I told her.

—Need what, missus?

—Yes. I'm going to my apartment. I have a very nice apartment by the park with nice furniture and everything. I lived there a very long time.

—Well now, that's real nice.

MARISA KANTOR STARK

I smiled at her. —I painted it myself, you know. I have
African violets. All different color flowers, pink, purple, white.

I was thinking maybe 1 can give her a cutting, a little plant
in a pot, and show her how to take care of it. I'll tell her be
careful no water on the leaves or they'll go rotten. But then
when I looked up she was gone. The bus was leaving without me.

Well, so that don't matter nothing, I can walk. I'm fine to
walk. To get to my apartment it's not difficult, it's by the park.

I got up from the bench and that's when I saw it. There on
the back what I didn't notice before, a black swastika. I felt hot
all over and then cold and I knew I couldn't leave it there. I
tried to rub it with a tissue, my hand was shaking so I could-
n't hardly hold it, but I stood for a long time rubbing and rubbing and still it wasn't coming off. All I can think is to put
something to cover it.

I don't have nothing with me, only my bag and my sweater,
and in my bag there wasn't too much. I was a little bit sorry
because it was my favorite sweater, the rose-colored one with
the little pulls at the elbow, but I taked it off and folded it carefully and hanged it over the back of the bench.

And now again I'm walking. It's all right, keep your eyes just
straight ahead. Not far now, it's by the park.

Then from very far away I heard a voice calling to me.
—Tanta! Tanta Maime!

Very slowly I looked around. It was him. My nephew, wearing a suit and tie, running down the street. He came up to me,
breathing hard, his shirt coming loose from his pants, his hair
going in all directions like it wasn't never combed. He stops
and grabs hold my shoulders. —Tanta.

—Oh, Milton. It's you.

—Thank God. Thank God I found you.

—I'm not lost, Milton.

He looks into my face. Now he looks angry. He shakes me a little bit. —What do you think you're doing? Just what in God's name are you doing here? Do you have any idea how dangerous this is?

—Don't be silly, it's not dangerous. I know this place, what can happen?

—I thought you had more sense, Tanta. They tell me you're in your room and then you're not there. We were looking everywhere, paging you, nobody's seen you, nobody knows anything. I came out . . . Tanta? Tanta, are you listening to me? Do you hear what I'm saying?

—Don't yell at me, Milton. I won't have you yell.

He stared at me for a minute then let go my shoulders and took my hand. —I'm not yelling. Come on, let's go back.

—I'm going to my apartment.

—Your apartment? There is no apartment, Tanta. You don't live there anymore, remember?

What's he telling me. What does he think I am.

—They're waiting for you, Tanta. For me to bring you back.

He starts to lead me to the corner. The bus is pulling to the curb. But I make my feet hard against the ground.

—Oh no. I know about you, Milton. Don't think I don't know what you're doing.

—What? What are you talking about?

—I'm not like that. I know exactly what you're taking me.—Tanta, I think you're tired. You don't know what you're saying. Listen, I want you to promise me something before we get on the bus. Promise you won't ever do this again.

—I don't make no promises.

MARISA KANTOR STARK

—You have to. This is very important. Promise me.

—I don't want to. I don't promise.

The bus driver honks his horn. —You folks coming or not?

He helped me up the steps, handed the driver a few dollars from his wallet. We sat down in the front seat. He's looking straight ahead. I look there too, at the way the driver has black hairs like little wires growing on his neck. He's not talking, I'm not talking.

I feel a chill on my arms. I fold them against my chest.

—Where's your sweater, Tanta? Don't you have a sweater?

—Somewhere, I don't know. I lost it.

—Here, take this.

He put his jacket over my shoulders.

❀　❀　❀

It must be six-thirty already. I can see through the glass into the dayroom, the people are getting up. The news is over, they're turning the television and starting to bring them to their rooms. In another minute they'll come for me, bring me my milk. They know I'm here.

Tomorrow they're getting me a new band for my wrist, Karyn said. —And you better not take it off this time.

I won't be surprised if there's no more a knife with my breakfast. I can see how it is, they'll want me to spread jelly on the toast with a spoon.

So long what they don't try to get me a beeper. I will not wear a beeper like Herman, like some kind of animal. That is the line. Because everybody has a line, there are some things a person can do and some things they can't do. And once you cross that line there's no way to go back.

You know, I'm thinking of something. It can happen that one day a lady will be walking with her bags and her feet gets tired. She'll want to stop and rest and there will be a bench. So she puts her bags down around her feet, between her legs nobody should take them, and leans back to close her eyes. Suddenly she feels something soft against her shoulders. It is my sweater.

She looks at it and wonders, that's funny, what's a sweater doing here. She'll touch it and it's soft and warm and such a pretty color pink, maybe she don't have nothing that color. Slowly she will take it and put it round her shoulders and sit that way, my sweater wrapped around her. And the wool will feel good against her skin and she won't be cold no more.

ABOUT THE AUTHOR

MARISA KANTOR STARK received her B.A. from Princeton in 1995 and her M.A. from Boston University in 1998. Her poetry and short stories have appeared in *Northeast Corridor, Circumference,* and the *Birmingham Poetry Review.* She is currently living in New York, where she is completing her second novel.

COLOPHON

This book was designed and typeset at Coffee House Press. The text face is Garamond, which is known for both its superior legibility and its graceful proportions. It is supplemented by the typeface Onyx, a Modern style of typographic design with sparkling contrasts of thick to hairline-thin geometric shapes. The paper is Glatfelter natural, which is acid-free and of archival quality. This hardcover original is part of a first printing in a first edition of 5,000.